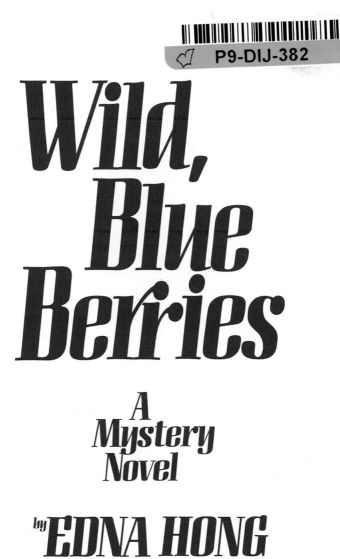

Wild, Blue Berries

A Mystery Novel

by EDNA HONG

AUGSBURG Publishing House • Minneapolis

WILD, BLUE BERRIES
A Mystery Novel

Copyright © 1987 Edna H. Hong

Scripture quotations unless otherwise noted are from the Revised Standard Version of the Bible, copyright 1946, 1952, and 1971 by the Division of Christian Education of the National Council of Churches.

Library of Congress Cataloging-in-Publication Data

Hong, Edna Hatlestad, 1913–
    WILD, BLUE BERRIES.

    I. Title.
PS3515.04974W5   1987   813'.54   87-9190
ISBN 0-8066-2274-1

Manufactured in the U.S.A.   APH 10-7190

1   2   3   4   5   6   7   8   9   0   1   2   3   4   5   6   7   8   9

Also by Edna Hong:

Bright Valley of Love
Forgiveness Is a Work as Well as a Grace
The Way of the Sacred Tree

One

They had met in the Bergen post office shortly after lunch—or dinner, as the local residents called the noon meal, for it was then they had their meat and potatoes. For some reason Paul found himself tilting to the vernacular of the year-around inhabitants of his parish. He did not know exactly why he had impulsively invited Dr. Lund, the retired physician and summer resident with the shaggy, gray hair, who carried both his weight and his years so well, to accompany him to the old, abandoned cemetery to visit the graves of his great-grandparents. Except, he thought, as they stood knee-deep in bracken in the graveyard, where every flower that was not an oxeye daisy was either a wild rose, a meadow buttercup, or a black-eyed Susan, except that he liked the old man. He was a good face in his congregation at St. Andrew, a face with keen eyes that watched him kindly, kind eyes that watched him keenly.

As they were looking at him right now, their owner gave every promise of being a good mentor to him in this, his first parish. And the probing question the kindly old man had just asked him did not contradict his first impression of the man. "Why did you accept the call to St. Andrew? I've been on several church call committees in my lifetime, Pastor, and I have observed at close hand the games some of you preachers play. So don't apostrophize to me about being called by the Holy Spirit. Were you perhaps lured by the best trout streams in Minnesota? Or was it because the dust of your venerable great-grandparents lies here in this abandoned cemetery?"

"My great-grandparents' dust may be venerable, but they themselves were far from venerable when they died." Paul knelt beside the two ancient tilted markers and traced the weather-worn inscriptions on the stained, once-white stones with his finger.

"Pastor Poul G. Amundson, 1885–1912. He was only 27 years old when he died. Margaret Amundson, 1891–1912. She was only 21."

"Nipped in the bud! Was it an accident or an epidemic?" the doctor asked.

"They mistook a poison berry for blueberries."

"Very likely the *Clintoni borealis* or blue-bead lily. A rather odd mistake, I must say. Are you sure that it wasn't deadly mushrooms? I've watched several mushroom deaths in my practice. They're not very peaceful."

"The story that has come down through the family jibes with the story I hear up here. They went blueberry picking and picked the wrong blue berries."

"Another one of these meaningless tragedies that lead some people to join the Order of the Nonbelievers! But your great-grandparents left their seed, for here you are, following in your great-grandfather's footsteps and even bearing his name. But you still have not answered my question, young man. Forgive my bluntness, but I really want to know why a promising, young Lutheran pastor like you chose to come to this parish on the fringes of everything. Not that I'm not glad that you did! You have all the makings of an excellent pastor. But it's rather lonely and isolated up here, especially when all of us summer residents, tourists, and hayfever escapees pack up at the end of August or early September and go home. In a way you may be burying yourself up here in the wilderness along with your great-grandparents."

"It may be lonely and isolated," chuckled Paul, rising to his feet, "but I assure you, Dr. Lund, that when you and all the other summer people, all you bearded professors and theologians and retired physicians and judges and lawyers, when you leave us in early autumn and carry away with you the weight of all your culture, knowledge, and education, the soul of our struggling little congregation here at St. Andrew will weigh no less than it did before you all left. To be perfectly honest, Dr. Lund, as I hope you will be with me, I would rather sit over a cup of coffee with old Nils and Tina Larson and talk about storms and shipwrecks on Lake Superior than discuss the state of the church with a bunch of you retired dignitaries. In fact, I was on my way to their home when I met you and had the sudden impulse to show you my great-grandparents' graves."

Whatever sharpness Paul's words seemed to have was made more bantering than barbed by the laughter in his lively blue eyes.

The older man looked up through his thick bifocals into the lean, tanned face with frank approval. "I'm glad you did, son! Please call me Toby. All my friends do. I didn't get to know you last summer when you were the summer youth chaplain up here on the Shore. I spent the summer in Sweden visiting relatives. I had such a good time that I stayed through Christmas. I lost my wife, Beth, two years ago and somehow couldn't face being up here alone without her last summer. I've heard nothing but good about you from the natives, and I liked the sermon you preached when you were installed two weeks ago. I've heard a good many preachers in my day, and the best thing some of them say is the Amen at the end of the final prayer. As for their prayers, most of them pray as if the Lord were thousands of miles away.

"But now you had better run along to Nils's and Tina's. I hope you will enjoy visiting me as well as you enjoy visiting them. I'm open to any subject you want to discuss—the geology and ecology of the North Shore or the psychology and pathology of its inhabitants and tourists. I'm an expert on almost anything related to these parts. Been coming up here since the Thirties."

"Thank you, Toby, for putting us on a comfortable first-name basis. Please call me Paul. I prefer first names on people as well as on plants. Incidentally, I knew you were an expert when you used two names for the blue-bead lily, and it didn't take me long to discover that Toby Lund is not exactly humble about being an expert."

"The two-name system is called binomial nomenclature, and it was developed by a fellow Swede, Linnaeus, who wasn't just a Latinist genius botanist, Paul. He must have believed along with his contemporary Christopher Smart that flowers are the poetry of Christ. Linnaeus is reported to have fallen on his knees and cried for joy the first time he saw the English heath covered with the yellow weed called furze. We don't have it up here in northern Minnesota."

"If Linnaeus the Swede and Christopher Smart the Englishman were alive today and were to visit the North Shore as tourists, they would probably be on their knees and in tears of ecstasy most of the time," Paul replied. "I would have to treat their prayer-worn knees as I used to treat the housemaid's knees of Swedish maidservants years ago. By the way, Paul, the blue-bead lily plant doesn't look anything like a blueberry plant. The blueberry is a low shrub with many branches. The blue-bead lily's leaves arch outward from a single stalk. I'm surprised that your great-grandparents confused them."

"Obviously they weren't Linnaeus or Lund!" Paul exclaimed.

"They must have been babes in the woods."

"Not so, Toby! Paul Gerhart Amundson and his wife were mature and marriageable, and they produced a baby that in turn became mature and marriageable, and in turn produced a baby that became mature and marriageable, and in turn produced twins—namely, me, Paul Gerhard Amundson the Second and my twin sister, Margaret O'Keefe Amundson, Maggie the Second."

"And Paul the Second is himself mature and marriageable, and his parishioners are wondering why he isn't married or about to be, and you may be sure that every marriageable girl between the Canadian border and Duluth has her eye on him!"

"As a matter of fact, I have—or had—an eye on one. I met her twice up here last summer and thought her the most beautiful girl I had ever seen. I am pretty sure that I was on the brink of love. At least, I felt differently about her than about all the other girls I thought I was in love with. Unfortunately, she seems to want a career more than she wants marriage."

"Well, well, well! Tell me her name, and I'll see what I can do. I have developed an affectionate great-uncle sort of relation with most of the young people along the Shore. What is the poor benighted creature's name?"

"I choose not to answer," chuckled Paul, "but before I leave you, I'll answer your first question, even though both are somewhat intrusive."

"I don't mean them to be."

"But before I answer your question, may I ask you an inquisitive question—one that every preacher would like to ask at least once in his or her lifetime? You say you have been on several church call committees. What led your committees to choose the pastors they eventually chose?"

"I really don't know," answered Dr. Lund, "for the committees I've been on never chose the pastor I wanted and voted for. They were looking for someone who combined all the spiritual, religious, moral, physical, and intellectual excellences in one package. They wanted a preacher, a pastor, a shepherd, a scholar, a theologian, a psychiatrist, a marriage counselor, an orator, an administrator, and a great number of other things, all under one skin. Once the choice came down to two men. One was six feet one, handsome, with a magnificently expressive face, charming, learned, dedicated, dignified. The other looked rather ordinary and uninteresting—a plump, dumpy Mickey Rooney, utterly unpretentious and unambitious for himself, quietly humble, irresistibly humorous. Of course the other was chosen. I was the only one who voted for Pastor Dumpy."

"Why did you?"

"Because I saw that he had no doors to his heart. Anyone and everyone could walk right in without knocking. But mostly because when he got into the pulpit and opened the Bible to the Gospel he was no longer plump, dumpy Pastor Average. He had pondered and penetrated that Gospel message so thoroughly during the week that it flowed out of him simply and naturally. Yet what he said was profound and went right to the soul—at least to my soul. He fed my soul, and that, in my opinion, is the primary function of a pastor. But as usual I am guilty of prolixity. Forgive me, and please answer my question."

"I don't mind prolixity at all if it's as uncommon and uncommonly intelligent and candid as yours, Toby. To answer your question, I accepted the calls to St. Andrew and to St. Luke at Good Harbor because the dust of my great-grandparents lies up here in the North Country, and because of the best trout streams in Minnesota, and because of the forests of black spruce and white birch that march almost to the Arctic Circle, and because of the wildness and wilderness, and because of the moose and the deer and the bear, and because of the ruffed grouse and the loons and the beaver, and because of the timber wolves, and because of the souls of the people who live up here, the souls of the natives as you call them, and because of the souls of the summer residents and the souls of the transient tourists, all of which souls have exactly the same soul needs, and because I feel that the sanctification of souls is as important as the cultivation of the mind and the satisfaction of the belly. And somehow I feel that his Holiness the Spirit has his soul-plucking fingers in all these causes and becauses. Therefore, Dr. Toby, I do in fact feel called by the Holy Spirit and moved by the Holy Spirit to accept the calls to St. Andrew and St. Luke. And I am not ashamed to confess that I continually thank my Creator that he placed within me the ears to hear that call in the red-tailed hawk and the bald eagle as well as the eyes to see it neatly typed in the letters of call I received from the two congregations. Now, have I answered your question? Are you satisfied, Sir Toby?"

"Thank you, Paul. Your answers are almost as prolix as mine. I hope we can share our prolixities again soon and often. I live in a log cabin on the point of Half-Moon Bay, your neighbor bay. Drop over sometime."

"Being your neighbor is a bonus. Incidentally, I chose to live here on Bergen Bay rather than in the somewhat ordinary parsonage in Good Harbor on the farthest street away from Lake Superior because I happened to find a wonderful log cabin begging for a tenant. It's furnished precisely to my somewhat primitive taste. I think the Holy Spirit had something to do with that as well. From my point I can see your Swedish flag flying with the American flag. It's a beautiful sight."

"I'm such a minority up here among the Norwegian fishermen and farmers turned resort and motel operators that I have to flaunt my honorable descent in some way. But you had better be on your way to Tina's and Nils's. I have a good murder mystery to get back to."

"Can you guess yet who dunit?"

"The clues are collecting like sea gulls around a dead lake trout washed up on the shore. Of course none of them as yet points to the one who really committed the crime. Incidentally, one of my favorite authors, G. K. Chesterton, says that a good sermon should be like a whodunit, even a trashy whodunit. The listener's attention should be excited. A sin has been committed. A sinner is at large. Who is he or she? Who dunit? The good sermon subtly narrows the possibilities, until finally the listener is forced to stop looking elsewhere for who dunit, but looks into his or her own heart and says, 'It is I! I—*I* am the sinner!' "

"The hardest words in all the world to say!" exclaimed Paul. "Nathan, the prophet, to King David, '*You* are the man, O King!' Only because David was brought to say, 'I, I am the guilty one,' could he come to God with that powerful prayer of confession and contrition. 'Against thee, against thee only, have I sinned.' "

"Psalm 51," said Dr. Lund.

"So you are a Bible expert, too!" laughed Paul. "That's a wonderful idea about a sermon being like a good whodunit, Toby. Tell me more about this G. K. Chesterton sometime."

"Better yet, read his books. I can lend you all of them."

Paul lingered at the graves.

Dr. Lund turned at the sagging, rusty iron gate. "Would you like me to come with my power mower and spruce up the cemetery?"

After a moment's thought Paul answered, "Thank you, no. I'll come with my shovel and straighten the tombstones, but I suspect that my great-grandparents would object to the wholesale murder your power mower would do in here. I have a feeling that they would rather have this wildflower garden around their graves than close-cropped grass or American Beauty roses. But you could replace the rusted-out hinges on that gate."

Alone at the graves, Paul whimsically wished that the ghosts of the dead really did take up residence at their tombstones. He had so many questions to ask them, so many wonderings. How did the Norwegian immigrant young man meet the Irish immigrant girl? Was it love at first sight, love so natural and overpowering in its naturalness that it wiped out all the unnatural barriers?

How else could a Norwegian Lutheran seminarian marry an Irish Catholic girl in the early 1900s, when Lutheran parents would rather have their son or daughter marry a heathen or a reprobate than a Catholic?

"Maggie O'Keefe," chuckled Paul, giving her tombstone a loving pat. "I wonder if the Lutheran powers that be insisted that you be rebaptized!"

Two

Despite the northeasters that sometimes swept across Lake Superior and hurled waves far ashore, shifting and shuffling pebbles and stones, stealing from and adding to beaches, the long, steel-reinforced-concrete public dock jutting into Bergen Bay had promised enough protection so that Nils Larson had dared to build his Norwegian-red cottage and boathouse close to the water. Yet he was a veteran of enough storms to protect the narrow beach with a row of huge boulders that blunted the force of the waves.

Approaching the house nested under a patriarchal balsam and a matriarchal birch, Paul felt as if he were paying a visit to Philemon and Baucis, the aged Phrygian couple who have become a symbol of a lifelong, lovelong marriage. Inside the house, the snowy-white lace curtains at the windows, the braided rag rugs, the two cherry rockers, the pictures in oval frames on the flowery wallpapered walls, the whatnot with little pitchers and fancy vases confirmed the impression.

But sitting at the dining room table in front of the wall of windows facing the sparkling bay, watching the sea gulls soar and dip, and drinking coffee and eating freshly baked bread, pickled herring, and strawberries still warm from the garden made him feel as if he were dining at the captain's table with the captain of the cruise ship the *S.S. Norway* and his good wife. He told Nils and Tina so, and they chuckled.

"When I was a boy in Norway—" Nils began.

"*Nayda!* Here we go again with Nils's 'when I was a boy in Norway' stories!" exclaimed Tina in mock exasperation. "You had better let me fill your coffee cup, Pastor. Nils's 'when I was a boy in Norway' stories can get pretty long. Have another slice of bread and some herring. Nils caught the herring last week, and I pickled it."

"See what I've had to put up with for over 65 years!" sighed Nils, looking at Tina fondly. "When I was a boy in Norway, I used to dream about being the captain of a big steamship. But we were poor fishermen. There wasn't a chance in the world then for me to even be the captain of a ferryboat."

"Ya, but Nils had his own fishing boat here on the lake," said Tina proudly.

"Shure ting! I had my own boat, and I had my own crew, too! Skipper, first mate, second mate, and the whole shebang."

"And every one of Nils's crew was named Nils Larson," giggled Tina.

"See what I've had to put up with for over 65 years!" sighed Nils.

Married for 65 years, and they're still teasing each other like newlyweds, thought Paul. *And they're not play acting for my benefit. The way they look at each other proves that!*

"When did you both come to America?" he asked, eager to hear more.

"I came in 1908 when I was 13," said Nils. "My mother and brother and I landed right at that there dock out there. My father came first and worked in a logging camp up on the Pigeon River. He liked this area because it looked so much like Norway, so he saved some money and got himself a homestead in Popple Valley, about five miles back in the woods, and sent for us. He met us right on that there dock. Oh, not that same dock. It's been rebuilt several times."

"When did you come, Tina?"

"I came in 1910 when I was 11. My father homesteaded a place in Popple Valley right next to Nils's father's place. Nils and I knew right away the minute we laid eyes on each other that we would get married some day. You never looked at another girl, did you, Nils?"

"Wel-l-l, now, I can't honestly say that! There was one I looked at pretty hard."

"Nils Johan Larson! You never said a word to me about this before!" sputtered Tina. Two red spots glowed in the cobweb of fine wrinkles on her cheeks.

"Every man and boy around here who had any manhood was in love with her. I wasn't the only one, Tina."

"*Now* you tell me!"

"Don't get excited, *Kjaereste!* She was already married. None of us could have her, and we all knew it. I tell you now only because her great-grandson is sitting here drinkin' coffee with us and lookin' so much like her that the old memories sort of get churned up again."

Paul set his just refilled coffee cup down so hard that the amber liquid spilled on the snow-white tablecloth.

"I'm sorry! What a clumsy fool I am! I'm terribly sorry!"

"Never mind," soothed Tina. "It'll come out in the wash. Even if I have a washing machine, I still boil all my whites."

"Tina has the whitest wash of anybody around here, and she's never used a drop of bleach."

"But I always use bluing, Nils."

"Bluing isn't bleach, Tina."

Tina patted Nils's cheek lovingly. "No, it isn't, and I wasn't *Fru* Pastor Amundson either. Nils, I don't mind at all your being in love with her. We girls all thought she was the most beautiful thing we had ever seen, and we all knew that you boys were wild about her. You *do* look like her, Pastor. The same thick, coppery red hair, the same blue eyes, the same high cheekbones, and a way with you that sometimes is more Irish than Norwegian."

"But Pastor looks like his great-grandfather, too, Tina. Your great-grandfather was so handsome, Pastor, that all the girls left us boys way behind in all the memory work he had us do in his summer Bible school. The girls were so smitten with him that—"

"Not me, Nils! I have never been smitten with anyone else but you, and you know it. Quit your teasing!"

"I never dreamed that I would ever meet people who had seen and talked with my great-grandparents!" marvelled Paul. "It never dawned on me that you two knew him. Please tell me everything that you can remember about them. Everything!"

"*Ta det med ro!*" said Nils, laying a gnarled hand on Paul's shoulder.

"He means 'Take it easy,'" said Tina. "Sometimes Nils forgets and uses Norwegian words."

"Ya," continued Nils, "take it easy, Pastor! We can't tell you much, you know. Your *oldefar*—"

"*Oldefar!*" repeated Paul. "Is that the Norwegian word for great-grandfather? I like it! How is it spelled?"

"O-l-d-e-f-a-r," said Tina. "Great-grandmother is *oldemor.*"

"*Oldefar* and *oldemor.* Beautiful words! That's what I'm going to call them from now on. Excuse me, Nils, I interrupted you."

"Your *oldefar* wasn't here with us in Bergen very long, Pastor. He came the summer of 1911 as a young seminary student to teach summer Bible school and preach. We didn't have a pastor then. He taught two weeks here in Bergen and two weeks down in Good Harbor. He came up here every third Sunday that summer and preached in the schoolhouse. He went up to the lumber camps at Pigeon River and preached a coupla times. You can yust bet that your *oldefar* was very popular with everyone. Farmers, fishermen, and lumberjacks—they all liked him. We had one preacher once who was terribly uppity. He was like some of the preachers back in the Old Country who thought they were a peg or two above the rest of us folks."

"But not your *oldefar!*" Tina chimed in. "There was nothing puffed up about him or *Fru* Pastor."

"Your *oldefar* was popular with all the young girls, too," continued Nils. "You can yust bet that every girl in Popple Valley and Bergen and Good Harbor under 18 went to summer Bible school that summer!"

"Did you, Tina?"

"Ya, shure. But Nils was more popular with me than your *oldefar!*"

"Tina was only 12," said Nils, "but she could say the books of the Bible faster than any of the older ones. Even faster than Helga Jenson, who was supposed to be the smartest one of all."

"I can still say them fast," said Tina. *"Første Mosebog, Anden Mosebog, Tredje Mosebog, Fjerde Mosebog, Femte Mosebog, Josuasbog, Dommernes bog, Ruths bog, Første Samuelsbog, Anden Samuelsbog, Første Kongebog, Anden Kongebog, Første Krønikebog*—See, I can still say them!"

Paul tipped back in his chair and shouted with laughter. "Seventy-five years! Two weeks of drilling on the books of the Bible, and you remember them 75 years later! That speaks well of my *oldefar's* teaching."

"Ya, but it speaks more about the young girls tryin' to make an impression on the young, unmarried seminary student," teased Nils.

"He was so popular with the congregations in both Bergen and Good Harbor that they made him promise that he would come back and be our pastor when he graduated from the seminary," said Tina.

"He came back the first of July in 1912," said Nils. "He came back with a wife and baby. They had been married in October, and the baby was born yust three weeks before they came up here. Pastor and *Fru* Pastor died the last week in August. So you see there's not much to tell. They weren't here very long."

"Don't forget to tell Pastor that *Fru* Pastor and the baby were a complete surprise to everyone up here. But after the first shock, everyone fell for them like a ton of bricks—just like they did the year before for your *oldefar*."

"Not everyone!" said Nils. "Not the women who had daughters old enough to get married. They wished he was still a bachelor."

"Ya, but Nils, you know that we girls saw right away that we couldn't hold a candle to *Fru* Pastor, and we were just glad that our wonderful young pastor had her for a wife—even if she wasn't a Norwegian and couldn't understand much Norwegian. Your *oldefar* was wild about her. He brought her along every time he came up here from Good Harbor with horse and buggy. It was almost as if they couldn't bear to be away from each other ever. We all thought it was wonderful to have the preacher's wife and baby along whenever he came. It was a wonderful time, but too short, too short! Such a shock it was! Such a shock!"

The three of them sat in silence and looked out the window.

Suddenly Nils stood up in his chair and pressed his face against the window. "Tina!" His voice trembled. "Tina, I think one is gone!"

"He's counting the baby mergansers," whispered Tina. "There's supposed to be 10 of them."

All three of them now stood at the window counting the darting, diving ducklings swimming after their mother.

"It's no use! They're scootin' on top of the water as if they've been scared. A hawk or some big fish has gotten one of them," said Nils, sinking heavily into his chair.

"Not so!" cried Paul. "There's Number Ten coming around your boathouse. See? He's joined the others, and his mother is scolding him."

"Let's go out and feed them that leftover *kringla*," said Tina.

When that had been done, Nils stood pensively watching the merganser family. "Our daughter wants us to sell this house and move to the Lutheran Nursing Home near Duluth so that we can be near her. But who would take care of our mergansers? They come back every year."

All the way back to his log cabin on the point Paul reflected on Tina and Nils. *It's really true what they say about happily married couples eventually resembling each other*, he thought. *Nils and Tina have been mated so long that they match, and not just in body, but in mind and spirit as well. What a wonderful relationship! The culmination of an inevitable and natural attachment. Proceeding smoothly through the stages of life. No leaping into relationship. No jumping in and out of relationship. A tender and simple idyll. A steady, trusting, wonderful growing in it—and into each other, until they are as alike as two drops of water. And yet so wonderfully their own individual selves!*

How I envy them, he thought, and found himself thinking of the daughter of the somewhat dour couple who came to St. Andrew every Sunday, although they now lived in Good Harbor. He supposed that the couple had grown up in the St. Andrew parish and, like many church members, retained their membership after they moved away, and drove many miles to attend the church services in the old church even if they lived two blocks from a Lutheran church in the new community.

Their daughter could easily have been my Maggie, he thought, but she had vanished last summer almost as quickly as she had appeared—only not before he had discovered that he was falling—or had fallen—in love with her. Suddenly she was gone, and she had never answered the two letters he had written to her at the Yale Graduate School of Nursing.

It occurred to him that his great-grandparents' relationship had been just the opposite of Tina's and Nils's. His great-grandparents apparently had been surprised by love. Theirs had been an unexpected leap into love, an unexpected leap into marriage, and very likely an unexpected leap into parenthood—and from all reports it had been an exceedingly happy relationship. But then at the peak of their happiness, that unexpected leap—into death!

Who or what, he wondered, determined the quality of a love relationship, whether it was a leap into love like his grandparents', or a slow, natural growing into love, like Tina's and Nils's? And how could a person tell the difference between being infatuated and being in love? And what would his own relationship of love be—if ever? Would love, sweet love, ever come to him? Would it surprise him some day? Would he be able to tell the difference between infatuation and true love? *Lord, Lord, keep me from being a lovesick fool!*

Three

The Fourth of July celebration at the public dock on Bergen Bay brought the whole Bergen community, with the exception of the bedridden and the misanthropes, together for a potluck picnic. Two families came early, built a bonfire on the shore with bleached driftwood, and prepared to plankroast an immense lake trout and a coho salmon. Another family brought a grill, built another fire, and prepared to fry hamburgers and roast dozens of wieners. Planks were laid across wooden sawhorses for tables, and bright tablecloths miraculously appeared from nowhere to cover them. The tablecloths, in turn, were soon covered with bowls of Jello and tossed salads, casseroles of baked beans, escalloped potatoes and ham, chicken and rice, tunafish and rice, baskets of homemade buns and breads, platters of cookies, pans of brownies and cakes, and every cream and fruit pie women's genius could turn out. Tina and some of the older Norwegian women brought platters of buttered and sugared lefse. A huge urn of coffee was brewed in the town hall across the highway and brought over to the dock. Crocks of Kool-Aid and lemonade, clinking with ice cubes, were transferred from car trunks to the long, makeshift table.

"What a production! Sheer fairy-tale magic!" exclaimed Paul to the women bustling around the table as he deposited his contribution to the potluck feast—a five-pound round of cheddar cheese and several boxes of Finnish rye crisp. "Do you remember the fairy tale of the magic tablecloth that in the twinkling of an eye could set out the most sumptuous banquet? I'll bet it couldn't match this miracle!"

"Be sure to eat hearty now, Pastor!" said one of the women mischievously. "It must be pretty slim pickin' at your house with no woman to cook for you."

"He may be a bachelor, but Pastor is a good cook," said another. "Haven't you heard? He had all the young people over last Saturday night, and they say he fixed the best pizza they've ever eaten."

"Are you sure it wasn't a Tombstone pizza made and frozen in Medford, Wisconsin?" asked one.

"Nope! Made it myself. From scratch," said Paul. "Scratch—it's a good cook's favorite ingredient, isn't it?"

"When are you going to invite us?" the women teased.

"As a matter of fact, I intend to have every group in both churches over to my cabin before my first year is out, and I intend to fix all the food myself. Would you women like to hold your next meeting at my cabin?"

He edged away from the table, pleasantly amused at their openmouthed amazement. He worked his way down the long dock, greeting people he knew from church by name and nodding at strangers. There were more of the latter than the familiar faces, and some of them looked like rather interesting characters. For some reason interesting characters seemed to be drawn to the shores of Lake Superior.

At the very end of the dock he saw a girl in jeans and a faded blue, cotton shirt and wearing dark glasses quietly gazing out across the lake. Ulla Fjelstad! The girl who had not answered his letters! No one else he knew wore her hair like that in a thick braid down her back and tucked under her belt. So she was home, then! For vacation? Waiting for a job? She was supposed to have graduated in June a full-fledged nurse practitioner from the Yale Graduate School of Nursing. Ulla Fjelstad. Although he had met her only a few times last summer, she was the only girl he could really say had ever fluttered his heart.

He stopped a step behind her and wondered why he should feel this strange physical exultation just looking at a girl's back and be stirred merely by the way her head sat on her neck and her neck sat on her shoulders. What a beautifully proportioned structure! Black hair that gleamed like a blackbird wing. Not a cold blue-black, but a warm black. Tendrils of it escaped her thick braid at the nape of her neck and curled against her fawn-colored skin. Or was it amber? Or umber? Umber-amber!

I'm looking at her only from behind, he thought, *and I already know that she's more wonderful than I remember her from last summer. Why? Is this the way* oldefar *felt when he first saw Maggie? Is this my love surprise? my leap? If so, why is it happening? Why does a fellow meet a thousand girls over the years and they are all like sparrows, and suddenly he sees one girl who is not a sparrow but a nightingale? Ulla Fjelstad, are you my nightingale?*

He stepped forward and leaned toward her left ear. "Tell me why you didn't answer my letters, or I'll push you off this dock, and when you come up and grab the end of the dock I'll stomp on your fingers."

Her eyelids, as much as he could see of them on the edge of the dark rims of her glasses, fluttered once in surprise, but she did not turn her head. "If you do," she murmured, "it will be the end of your career as a pastor at St. Andrew."

"I'm not as career-minded as you seem to be, Miss Fjelstad. Is that why you did not answer my letters?"

When she turned, he did not step back, and she was forced to speak to his nose. "Please! This is not the time and place!"

He edged closer. "Tell me a time and place, or in you go."

"I really think you would!" she gasped.

"I would indeed," he said, edging still closer. "How about Monday, preacher's holiday?"

"Pastor Amundson! Pastor Amundson!" someone called from the middle of the dock. "They want you to ask the blessing before we eat."

Ah, yes. He had been warned by older pastors that whenever a public gathering seemed to call for a pious nod in the direction of the Deity, he as a clergyman would be called upon to do his pious duty. One seasoned clergyman had even advised him for the sake of ecumenicity to address his prayer only to a Supreme Being and to pray in such general terms that no one could take offense. "Be like the apostle for whom you are named. The apostle Paul prided himself on being all things to all men, a Greek to the Greeks, a Jew to the Jews."

Paul relished remembering that he had snapped back to the venerable Pastor Prudent: "And an agnostic to the agnostics, an atheist to the atheists, an anti-Christian to

the anti-Christians, an antichurchian to the antichurch-
ians?"

The crowd milling on the dock parted to allow him
to proceed through to the table, where the two fish now
rested in their savory juices. Dr. Lund plucked at his
elbow as he passed and muttered, "You know what I
think about invocations. Try not to be banal."

*Banal or not, let me not try to be a crowd pleaser! Or a Toby
Lund pleaser. Or, for that matter, an Ulla Fjelstad pleaser,*
Paul thought as he stepped up on a solid camp stool
someone handed to him and looked out over the crowd
of some hundred people and waited for them to be quiet.
His eyes went beyond the faces looking at him and waiting for his blessing of the food, to Lake Superior, sen-
suously stretched out to the sun's completeness like a
lovely woman sunbathing. Where the bay met the open
water two sailboats sailed in a shimmering haze.

A boyish smile suddenly lit Paul's face. "When we ask
a blessing or give thanks, we as a rule duck our heads
and close our eyes and mumble some words over meat
and potatoes. Let's do it differently today! Please turn
around, all of you. Look away from me. Look at that
beautiful fresh-water lake out there—the largest, the
deepest, and the most beautiful in the world. Let's begin
by thanking God for the blessing of it. Keep your heads
up and your eyes on it as we pray.

"Thank you, God of all creation, for creating this blessing, this provider of food for our tables, this water road
to the whole world, this feast for our eyes. Lord God of
all creation, we thank you for creating Lake Superior."

"It wasn't God!" a voice muttered. "It was the ice age
and the glaciers that created the Great Lakes."

An angry murmur rose from the crowd. Paul briefly
focused his eyes on a young, bearded man standing a

few feet in front of him and beside a girl with long, uncombed blonde hair. *Ah, a couple of antiestablishment kids who have come for a free feed,* Paul thought. *Why did all the radical young people look alike, like unmade beds, ostentatiously sloppy? Back to first principles—sandals and simplicity. Well, if they think they can raise my hackles, they will be disappointed. Forgive me, Lord, for the showing off I'm about to do!*

Paul's voice continued steadily. "We thank you, Lord of all creation, for creating the ice age that created the glaciers that formed the ancestors of Lake Superior— Lake Keweenaw, Lake Duluth, Lake Minong, Lake Houghton, Lake Nipissing. We thank you for abolishing the ice age and leaving behind this lake we now know and love and call Lake Superior. We thank you, Father of all humankind—"

"Why Father? Why not Mother?" A woman's voice, belligerent. The girl with the uncombed hair. Perhaps one of those ferocious female grammarians who want to rewrite the Bible and change the gender of the Deity.

Woman, it's true that you women have suffered male tyranny, but beware that you yourself do not become a tyrant! Lord, Lord, guard my lips right now from being flippant! Paul prayed silently.

Paul's voice proceeded smoothly and evenly. "God, we thank you for creating Wisdom first of all your creation and for establishing her as the feminine principle. We thank you for creating all things together with Wisdom. We thank you for creating the first human beings to live on these shores, the darkskins who loved this land and these waters and cared for them better than we whiteskins have done. Today, especially, we thank you for the freedom, the Fourth of July freedom, that allowed our ancestors to come freely to these shores, to work out a living, a good living, in this freedom. Grant that we here today may preserve this freedom and live in peace with each other. In the name of your Son, who made us free with a greater freedom than our Fourth of July freedom, and who did potluck miracles with five loaves and three fish, and whose miracles never cease. Amen."

Paul quickly edged his way to the bearded young man and the girl with the uncombed hair before some of his well-intentioned parishioners might angrily accost them. Not, however, before one of the parishioners said loudly enough for the two to hear, "Don't pay any attention to them, Pastor. They're just here for a free lunch."

Paul put a hand on each one's shoulder. "I'm happy to meet you two—a geologist and a theologian. Two of my favorite subjects, geology and theology. I'd like to talk with you about them sometime soon."

"There isn't anything in the Bible about Wisdom being a feminine principle," the girl said sullenly. "You made that up. The Bible is the most male-chauvinist book ever written!"

"Oh, but I didn't make it up at all, dear lady! Wisdom was, is, and forevermore will be a lady! I made a special study of her to refute the charge that the Bible is a male-chauvinist book. Studied both the canonical and the books that have been in and out of the canon through the years. Ecclesiasticus, which has always been accepted by the Catholics, says it the best:

> Wisdom was created before all things,
> . . . The Lord himself created wisdom;
> he saw her [*her*, please note!] and apportioned her,

he poured her out upon all his works.
She [*she*, mind you!] dwells with all flesh
according to his gift, and he supplied her
to those who love him.

"Isn't that amazing?" Paul exclaimed. "If Ecclesiasticus doesn't satisfy you, read the 10th chapter of the Wisdom of Solomon. A great hymn of praise to Wisdom, and always addressed to Wisdom as a female. Always *she, she, her, her!* Christ himself personified Wisdom as a woman when he said, 'Wisdom is justified by all her children.' The book of Proverbs time and again refers to Wisdom: 'She is more precious than jewels, and nothing you desire can compare with her.' Indeed, my friend, those early male patriarchs could not have made it without her, Wisdom, the Feminine Principle!"

The young man pulled the girl roughly away. Behind them stood Ulla, who had apparently heard Paul's whole totally unplanned rhapsody on female Wisdom. There was a quizzical, puzzled look on her face. She had not taken off her dark glasses, but at least she was not wearing her buttoned-up look.

"Will you share potluck with me?" Paul asked her.

"Why not?" she said. Paul rejoiced to see the girlish openness of her face. To his amazement he found himself wondering how soon he dared ask her to share a potluck future with him. Why not? Why not be as speedy as his great-grandparents? They had played the music of their love *allegro*, not *andante!*

Four

Paul saw Ulla again at the convivial coffee hour after the worship service on Sunday. He had ceased to wonder about the properness of these jovial coffee hours after Sunday worship services and to question whether this was or was not holy hilarity. Could genuine geniality and good spirits ever be anything but holy?

Ulla was not wearing her dark glasses today, but her face had the zipped-up look again. Was it because she was flanked by her parents, whose faces were also closed doors? Paul wondered. *Who are you, anyway, loveliest of girls? You are here but not here. You grew up here; your roots are here. So why are you not here?*

When Ulla's parents went to refill their coffee cups, Paul approached her. "What shall we do with preacher's holiday tomorrow?" he asked.

"That's for you to decide."

"My instant decision is that you take me to your favorite spot, wherever it may be," Paul said.

"I'll meet you at the post office at ten o'clock."

"May I not pick you up at your home?"

"I don't like to be picked up. Wear your oldest clothes and tennis shoes. My favorite place is remote and ruthless."

As are you this morning, Paul thought as Ulla released her hand from his strong clasp and moved toward the door. Obviously she did not want him to come to her parents' retirement condominium in Good Harbor.

He extended a hand to pat the head of a towheaded lad who could not shake hands because his fists were full of cookies. It pleased the congregation that he knew them all, even the children, by name. What they did not need to know was that he rose early on Sunday and studied the rather recently published St. Andrew church directory with all the names and pictures. In color. Like Mrs. Alexon, for example, in her shocking pink suit. The portly summer resident from Chicago was steering in full sail toward him, wearing the same shocking pink pants suit she was wearing in the picture. Although she was not a member, she had been coming to the Shore for so many summers that she wanted to be included in the directory.

"Good morning, Mrs. Alexon," he said, and wondered once again if he studiously memorized all these names in order to please the parish. Perish the thought! A plague on all his self-doubts! A person's name was like a doorknob. It opened the door to knowing another person. And was that thought in turn his self-justifying self justifying itself? *Good Lord, deliver me from my self and my self-reflecting!*

"Good morning, Tina and Nils," Paul said, cupping both their hands in the cup of his own. He did not try to disguise the extra warmth in his voice. *Oh, Tina and Nils,* he thought, *your faith is so living and so simple and so natural that you don't even know how you got it! And I'll bet that there isn't a cloud in it.*

Dr. Lund had no greeting save a terse mutter as he brushed by. "Banal you are not!"

Nor are you, my friend, Paul mused. *A man with dogma and tradition that he had never allowed to fossilize. Blessed are the orthodox who have never lost the romance and adventure of orthodoxy!*

The Bergen post office is all that there is to Bergen, save for a bar at the next crossroad, a town hall across from the public dock, and the Lutheran church around the bend and up the hill going south—or southwest, to be correct. Paul found it difficult to dislodge the notion that the shore of Lake Superior ran straight northward rather than northeastward. At ten o'clock in the morning the post office is peopled only by the postmistress. People who live off the mail route come at one o'clock, after the mail is sorted, to pick up their mail and exchange local news.

Paul walked the half mile from his cabin at the southeast point of Bergen Bay, wondering all the way why Ulla had not suggested picking him up there. Would that have intimated more intimacy in their relationship than she wanted, or cared to admit? Or did she, too, think he was nuts to live out there on the point instead of in the spacious parsonage the two congregations provided in Good Harbor. But that house was as far from the lake as it could be and still be in town limits! Well, nutty or not, the congregations were not losing money on his passion for living right on Lake Superior, surrounded on three sides by water. They had rented the parsonage to the new lawyer in the area for $200 more a month than they had to pay for the rent of his cabin. What a find, that solidly built and fully furnished to his primitive taste log cabin! He hoped that the recently deceased childless widower who had built it and lived in it for many years somehow knew in his afterlife, his after-earth-life, that his beloved house had passed into the possession of someone who loved it as much as he had. As soon as he had paid his college debts, he would buy the cabin for his own. Even if he moved away to some other parish—perish the thought!—it could be his vacation home. And Ulla's?

Precisely at ten Ulla drove into the post office parking lot in an orange Toyota pickup. She was dressed exactly as she had been on the Fourth—faded jeans, flannel shirt, dark glasses, shuttered face, and all.

"Hi! I like your carriage," Paul said, "Is it yours?"

"*She,* not it. She's my only possession, and her name is Henna. Not Hannah. Henna. You know, the color some women's hair gets when they try to dye it themselves and it gets tootoo orange. Henna moved me and all my books and things from New Haven here."

"Where is Henna going to move you and all your books and things next?"

"I don't know yet. Minneapolis, maybe. But I'd rather go west. The state of Washington attracts me because it's so much like the North Shore."

"Do you have any calls?"

"What do you mean? Job leads? Telephone calls begging me to set up a nurse-practitioner practice in Walla Walla?"

She looked at him with amusement. "Only preachers receive the kind of call you received. Nurse practitioners don't get called by the Holy Spirit."

"Don't be so sure about that! I happen to believe that the Holy Spirit does a lot more calling than we think he does. I believe that the sewer and drainage guy from Good Harbor who pumped out the septic tank at my cabin was called by the Holy Spirit, for he so obviously enjoys his work and does it so well. After his visit I almost preached a sermon on the solid waste of sin and pride and how it plugs up the channels of our beings— ending the sermon, of course, with the gospel of forgiveness that unplugs the plugs, unstops the stoppage, and gets the pipes and sewers freely flowing again."

"You would! You would!" Ulla's voice quivered with laughter. "I can hear your closing prayer. O, Great Architect of the Public Works we call the world, forgive our polluted ways. And when we are admitted to the Final Inspection, sweep us into your presence without an impact study."

Good heavens, the girl certainly is not suffering from malnutrition of the imagination! Paul thought. "Not bad! May I enlist your help in writing my sermons?" he chuckled.

"Where is Henna taking us?" he asked as the pickup turned into the Trout River State Park, "Aha! to the Kettles of the Trout River. I was there with a youth group from St. Paul last summer. So that's your favorite spot in all the world."

"Positively not! The Kettles are too public!" she exclaimed as they got out of the car. "This is only the starting place to where we are going. It's a rather grueling path that eventually becomes pathless. Are you up to it, Preacher man?"

"You are speaking, ma'am, to a former Outward Bound guide. But before we start, why don't you remove your dark glasses? Why hide the loveliest of eyes? Why

36

hang hostile signs in front of your windows to your inner being? Keep Out! Do Not Enter! Leave Me Alone! No Trespassing!"

"What if I don't want trespassing in my inner being?" she asked soberly. But she removed the glasses and tossed them into the driver's seat. "As long as we're divesting, you had better shed your watch and your billfold and keys and whatever else a man carries in his pockets. They might get wet or lost today. I'll lock them in the cab. Okay! Are you a runner?"

"I don't run in people-packed marathons, but if this is going to be a doublethon, I'm game."

"Then we'll run the path to the Kettles. It's only three miles."

She set so fast a pace, and the stony path, varicose-veined with roots, demanded such alert attention that he had to ignore the river tumbling on his left to Lake Superior from Minnesota's highest elevation. Like all the other rivers on the North Shore, the Trout is a white-water river, pied with froth. The symphony of its sound interwove with the steady beat of his feet and the singing air to produce a state of euphoria. He wondered if that lithe and lissom slip of humanity ahead of him was feeling the same jubilation. Backs do not reveal much, but her thick black braid worked loose from her belt and was dancing.

They passed an elderly couple on the path, and at the Kettles, where the more or less established path ended, they encountered a pair of frantic parents trying to instill in their wild and willful children their own fear of heights and plunging water.

"Let's push on," Ulla said. "This will be the toughest part. Sure you want to keep on?"

Was she twitting or taunting him? Paul wondered. What kind of a game was she playing with him? Whatever, he jolly well would not turn back! He bounded after her.

After they had left the faint semblance of an unestablished path fishermen had made and marked with discarded cigarette packs and candy wrappers (*the white man's way of marking the path,* he thought ironically), they had to struggle through thickets of alder and hazel brush. Or take to the river. Wherever the river widened and was conveniently strewn with boulders, Ulla rock-hopped, bounding from one exposed stone to the next with unerring instinct.

"Watch out for the loose ones!" she called.

"How can you tell?"

"You can't."

The river narrowed again, and the stepping stones went under water. Back to the bushes again. And so it went. On and on. One hour. Two hours.

Confound her! Paul exclaimed under his breath. *What is the little she devil trying to do? Is she making this a male-female contest? Malevolently trying to humble the male sex by proving her superiority over him, its representative? So be it! This representative of maledom will not peter out!*

That colloquialism, peter out. What, he wondered, *was its origin? Does it trace back to the apostle Peter? The rock that sometimes splintered? I'll have to investigate that when I get back to my books. Could be good sermon material there. Meanwhile, my lovely antagonist, this male is not going to peter out, cave in, fizzle out!*

He suddenly realized that he was no longer fighting his way through thickets but was on a narrow ascending path.

"It's an animal path," she called. "It gets pretty steep."

Steep! It is practically perpendicular! Paul decided. But he doggedly kept at her heels, although she warned him about pebbles and small stones her feet might dislodge. The sun was directly overhead now, and by the time they reached the top, they were both drenched with sweat. He had to wipe the sweat from his eyes before he could see where they were. The blood pulsed in his temples, and a cut on his left cheek from a branch stung painfully.

"This," she said quietly, "is my most favorite spot in the world. It's the deer's most favorite spot, too, as you can see from all the droppings. I am sure that they come here for no other reason than just to look."

They were standing at the top of a steep gorge, its rock face stained with bright orange lichen. A hundred feet below, the Trout River cascaded in an S-shaped series of waterfalls. At the wide beginning of the canyon, the river divided and subdivided and flowed over a wide expanse of table-top-smooth black basalt. The streams united, narrowed, and rushed between the narrow walls of the gorge. At the end it entered a deep basin, bordered on the far side by a flat upthrust of the canyon floor. After a long silence Paul whispered, "It's worth it! It's worth every bead of sweat and every scratch. Thank you for bringing me here."

She turned from the gorge and smiled up at him, a completely guileless and childlike smile. "I'm glad you like it! Somehow I knew you would!"

He caught his breath. *Ulla, this is you! You think you are showing me your most favorite spot in the world, but you are revealing your true self to me.*

"Did I pass the test?" he asked quietly. "Do I receive an award? A blue ribbon, or at least a red one? If you have no blue or red ribbon, a kiss will do."

Her face slammed shut. She backed swiftly away, re-treated down the edge of the cliff a dozen or so yards. Then with a bound she ran to the edge of the cliff and leaped far out. Her body plummeted down, down, down, and her long braid soared in the air like the tail of a kite.

"No!" Paul cried in horror. "Ull-a-a-a, *no!*"

Five

Ulla's head bobbed up out of the river's basin at the end of the gorge. "Come on in!" she called up to him. "The water's fine. Jump off where I did, right between the stunted cedar and the twisted birch."

His horror swiftly turned to anger. The reckless she devil! What would she do next to try to diminish him? He descended to the stunted cedar. Without a second look downward he backed up, took a running leap, and dropped like a stone, wondering all the while if his body would land on rocks or on top of her, and would their deaths be called a double suicide? How would people know that it was a murder—she the murderer and he the victim? Instinctively he kept his feet tightly together. They cut the water and split it open for his body to enter, but the water, tenacious to cohere, acted like an air cushion against his descent. His feet hit bottom more like a rubber ball than a stone, and his body bounced back up to the surface.

Exhilaration replaced anger as swiftly as anger had replaced horror. Wow! He had done a Daniel Boone stunt! He had just done what he had always fantasized doing in the days when he read about Daniel Boone escaping from the Indians by leaping off a cliff into a river. His eyes measured the sheer drop. Forty feet at least! *Deo gratias!* He shivered involuntarily at the thought of hurtling anywhere but into the deep center of the basin.

But after he swam across the pool, climbed to the flat upthrust of the bedrock of the canyon, and stood face-to-face with her, his anger returned redoubled. He grabbed her drenched and dripping shoulders and shook her violently. "Don't you ever do that to me again!"

"I should have told you that I've jumped off that cliff ever since I was 12 years old," she said remorsefully.

His hands dropped to his side. "You grew up near here?"

"My great-grandparents' homestead in Popple Valley is nearby. During the Depression my grandparents moved back there with their son, my father, and lived with great-grandmother. My grandfather died quite young, and grandmother and my father kept on living there. The place is abandoned now, but I spent many summers here before that happened. I know this area as intimately as you, I suppose, know your Bible. I can find the beaver dams on the creeks flowing into Trout River as easily as you can find your favorite psalms. I know every clump of blue iris within a half dozen miles in any direction."

"I can't be as boastful as that about knowing my Bible," laughed Paul. "There's a woman in the Bible study group at Good Harbor who I am sure is trying to embarrass me on that score. She asked me a question about a reference to Sheol in Habakkuk and watched me very closely to see if I had any trouble finding the book. The old girl was putting the new preacher to a test, just as you were, Riddle Girl!"

Paul put his hand under Ulla's chin and lifted her face. "Look at me, Ulla, and don't lie to me! I'll bet your great-grandparents' homestead is no more than a 20-minute walk from here by an easy path down to the river. Furthermore, the alder thickets, I finally decided, are usually just narrow strips along streams. If we had gone up from the river a little, we wouldn't have had to fight our way through those dense clumps. So I ask you, Ulla. Are you a brazen little minx trying to test me? Are you thinking that preachers are an emasculated lot, and you want to prove your point by watching me flunk out? Do you hate men in general and me in particular?"

She tried to turn away, but he clasped her head between his hands. "No, you don't! You are not going to get away by jumping into the river this time."

"Unhand me, then, and I'll tell you. But you won't like it."

"That's for me to decide," Paul replied.

"I don't want to look at you when I tell you. Let me turn my back."

"Turn your back."

She turned, forced her hands into the pockets of her sodden jeans. After a long silence, she said, "I suppose in a way I was testing you and hoping that you would flunk. Since I met you last summer, I have talked with you no more than twice. But I liked you. I was drawn to you in a way that I've never been drawn to a man—to anyone, for that matter."

"Then why didn't you answer my letters?"

Her shoulders tensed under the wet, clinging shirt. "I sensed that you felt the same way about me, and I did not want to lead you on to think anything could come of a relationship between us."

"Why not?"

She whirled about and pounded his chest with her fists. "Because I don't believe in marriage, that's why! I have yet to see a happy marriage—just *one* happy marriage. *Really* happy, I mean! The marriages I see are either terribly sad or terribly bad. Marriage destroys love, and I don't, I won't let myself fall in love and see it destroyed by marriage. I won't get bogged down in the swamp of married life. I won't! I won't!"

Her fists were beating a wild tattoo on his chest now. Paul seized her wrists and held them firmly. "If you don't believe in marriage, do you believe in meaningful relationships?"

"Now you're being sarcastic! No, I don't believe in meaningful relationships either. I see no difference between falling out of love in marriage or falling out of love in a so-called meaningful relationship. Either way is the ruin of love."

"At least the live-in partners are not doomed to a lifetime of hell, an ice-cold hell where all the fires have died," he said, releasing her wrists.

She looked at him in surprise. "So you admit that what I say is true?"

"I am quite aware that marriage doesn't enjoy high prestige at present. As for what you just said, there are bits and pieces of truth in it. When I was filling pulpits around the Twin Cities during my seminary days, I once attended a golden wedding reception. For a time I stood beside the rather tame-looking, golden groom and congratulated him on 50 years of wedded bliss. He leaned close and whispered, 'Pastor, they were 50 years of hell!'

"As I said, there are bits of truth in what you say, but as truth, what you say is as warped a truth as I've heard, and I mean to find out who or what warped your perception of marriage. But not right now. Right now I'd like to shed these clammy clothes, hang them to dry on this dwarfed birch tree, and swim. That pool looks inviting—from *this* height."

"Shall I turn my back?" she asked mischievously.

"Not again," he laughed. "I'll stop with my purple shorts, and I'm sure your bra and panties are much more decent than a lot of bikinis I've seen. If your dear, darling deer are standing up there on their lookout point watching us, they won't see anything to flick their white tails about. I'm not going to seduce their lovely friend. In fact, Ulla, I'm not going to try to kiss you or ask you for a kiss. If there's any kissing, you'll have to ask for it. But," his voice dropped its bantering tone and became quietly sober, "but I'm never going to stop telling you that I love you, and I'm never going to stop trying to unwarp that ugly warp of yours."

"Ugh! You make me sound humpbacked!"

"Maybe your psyche *is* humpbacked. That's not to say mine is unblemished. Now, may one dive headfirst from here? Any hidden boulders to break my neck and make me a paraplegic for life?"

"None whatever," she said, jackknifing into the pool.

Paddling around Paul a bit later, Ulla said, "I appreciate what you just said up on the rock."

"What in particular?"

"What you said, or meant to indirectly say, I sup-

45

pose—that you weren't going to arouse me and entice me and win me with all the usual erotic approaches."

She dove under him and came up on the other side. "Because," she said impishly, "I don't think it would be very difficult to do. You *did* pass the test swimmingly."

This time she dove under him and came up 15 feet away.

"Ulla," he called. "Ulla, I love you, I love you, I love you! I'll shout it to the cliffs, to your friends the deer, to the bear and the moose and the fish and the butterflies and the dragonflies and the water bugs."

"How about the bloodsuckers and the lampreys?"

"To them, too! I shout it to all creation. Ulla, *I love you!*"

For an hour or more they dove, swam, tested their strength against the currents, explored the numerous miniwaterfalls, found the ledges behind them where they could hide from each other.

"It's another Daniel Boone stunt," he cried in boyish delight. "Wow, two of them in one day! He escaped from the Indians once by diving off a cliff and another time by hiding behind a waterfall."

"Legends, I'll bet. The Indians would have dived right after him. They weren't so dumb that they wouldn't have looked behind waterfalls."

"Come, come, Ulla. Don't destroy my most cherished folklore!"

Dressed again in their sun-warmed clothes, they walked the faintly discernible path from the gorge to the doorless, windowless, shingleless, mouse-colored husk and hulk of a house in Popple Valley. Grass grew through the broken boards of the stoop.

"My most unfavorite spot," she said gloomily.

"Who or what brought it to this state so fast?" he asked in puzzlement.

"Vandals," she answered. "We grow them in the wilderness, too. Unspoiled nature doesn't always create unspoiled human beings."

When Paul made a move to go into the house, Ulla said, "I don't like ghosts. And please don't poke into my past. I don't want to spoil a wonderful day. I don't feel like talking about it—my past, that is. In fact, I don't feel like talking at all."

"Neither do I," Paul said. He felt like taking her hand as they walked along, but didn't. *You feel it, too,* he mused—*the dizzy, sweet mystery of love. The difference between us is that you fear it and I don't. You fear that marriage will chase away all the mystery, and I believe that marriage shields and treasures it.*

Out on the narrow gravel road at the end of the hardly perceptible lane he stopped and looked at her quizzically. "I have a feeling that it's about five miles to the lake and five or six more miles to your car in the Trout River State Park. I also suspect that only a lone fisherman ever travels this road now that everyone has left Popple Valley and moved down to the Shore."

"Your feelings and suspicions are quite on target," she said.

But a lone fisherman did come along, picked them up, and obligingly deposited them beside Henna at the state park.

When Henna had deposited him at his cabin door, he leaned on the driver's window. "Preacher's holiday is over," he said, "and you made this one memorable. Tomorrow I have an errand to do at Nils and Tina Larson's. I wish you would go along with me. Will you?"

"Why?" she asked.

"I want you to observe a happy marriage at close hand."

Six

Ulla called early the next morning to say that she would run from Good Harbor to Nils's and Tina's cottage on Bergen Bay.

"Ten miles?" Paul exclaimed. "I just read an article—"

"Yes, I know," she interrupted. "Jogging has lost its chic. Moderation is in. Even Jane Fonda has switched to the slow lane. But I can think of nothing better to do on a warm and sunny morning with a clean wind off the lake than run 10 miles. I'll be running, sir, not jogging! *Jog* is a mongrel word. The mother word is *jot*, meaning jolt, and the father word is *shog*, meaning shake. Running is a flowing."

"How long will it take you to flow to Bergen Bay?"

"I'll meet you there in two hours."

Paul found Ulla kneeling with Tina over a cluster of

bluebells. Her cheeks were still glowing from the 10-mile run.

Berry-black eyes, cheeks like wild roses, he thought, and at the same time he wondered at how swiftly love descended and changed a person's whole life. *Descended? No question of it! Where but from above could something so wonderful come?*

"They're the first bluebells I've seen in blossom this year," Ulla told him excitedly when she heard his step. "They're my favorite flower. What's yours?"

"Taraxacum officinale."

"Never heard of it," she said.

"It's a golden-yellow flower that gets its common name from its toothed leaves. The French call it *dente-de-lion.* If one translated that directly one would call it lion's tooth, but we've just adulterated the French and call it—"

"Dandelion!" she laughed, rising to her feet. "I walked right into that trap! I won't ask why it's your favorite flower, or we'll get a long sermon on 'The Uncommonness of the Common' or 'The Extraordinariness of the Ordinary' or 'The Dandelion as a Symbol of Ecumenicity.' We don't want sermons on Tuesday, do we, Tina?"

Ulla bent to help Tina to her feet. Paul stooped to take her other arm.

"It's my rheumatism," Tina apologized. "I guess they call it arthritis these days. No, we don't want sermons on weekdays."

"That reminds me of an Irish folktale I once read about a kind old peasant who did a fairy a good turn and was given two wishes," said Ulla. "First he wished for a month of Sundays. Nobody could do a lick of work. The taverns were closed. The whole village had to go to church and hear sermons every day. By the end of the first week everyone hated the poor man. I'm sure they hated the preacher, too. Anyway, the poor man had to use his second wish to undo the first one."

"What's all that *sniksnak* out there?" grumbled a voice from the open window. "Can't a fella get a decent sleep in his own house?"

"He's only teasing," said Tina. "He's been sleeping a whole hour. Come in, you two. This morning I baked Princess Astrid's *kringla*. The recipe is in the *Nordmans-Forbundet* magazine. We'll see if it is any better than my *kringla*."

Nils greeted Paul with a strong handshake and Ulla with a bear hug that left her gasping.

"So you are old friends!" exclaimed Paul, remembering with chagrin his invitation to Ulla to make this visit with him to observe a happy marriage at close hand. How stupid to forget that she had grown up with the people in this parish!

"Old friends!" chuckled Tina. "I held Ulla when she was baptized. She's our godchild."

"Godchild?"

"Ya, I know," said Nils. "Tina and I were too old for that. The pastor told Ulla's pa that, too. He said Ulla should have young godparents who could bring her up in the Lord and not die on her before she reached the age of—what's the word I'm lookin' for?"

"Discretion," said Ulla. "I'm not so sure I've reached it yet, godpapa and godmama."

"But Ulla's pa said if we couldn't be the godparents, Ulla wouldn't be baptized. He's sort of ornery. Stubborn as a mule."

"Stubborn as his Grandma Lissi," said Tina.

"Ulla's pa doesn't have many friends, but he's always liked me," continued Nils. "We fished together. Still do sometimes. So the pastor had to give in, and we stood up for Ulla."

"And then," chuckled Tina, "then we went and lived longer than all the young ones that could've stood up for her."

"That reminds me of a very interesting Eastern Orthodox understanding of the godparent-godchild relationship," said Paul. "I learned about it when I was doing a paper in seminary on that branch of the Christian church. The Eastern Orthodox regard the godfamily relationship as spiritual and closer than the flesh-and-blood relationships. Nils and Tina, if you were Orthodox and not Lutheran and lived some time ago, none of your grandchildren could marry Ulla. It would be regarded as incest. As a matter of fact, even to be confirmed together prohibited a boy or girl from marrying.

"I'm not advocating a return to that understanding, but I wish that Lutherans would have preserved some of the feeling of the sacred responsibility of the godparent, godfamily relationship. I don't even know who mine are. Someone in Chicago, I suppose. I was born there, but my parents lived there only two years, and those friends seem to have dropped out of their lives. I would like to know them, the whole god-clan—god-sisters, god-brothers, god-uncles, god-aunts, god-cousins, everybody!"

Nils and Tina, meanwhile, were looking at each other and sharing some secret mirth.

"Come on, godpapa! Please tell us the joke," pleaded Ulla.

"It's a good thing they didn't think that way when Tina and I was growing up or we'd never have gotten married. Tina and I was confirmed together. Tina, maybe you and I are guilty of an awful sin!"

"Not carnal," said Paul. "Spiritual—but only according to older Orthodox thinking. Don't worry, you haven't been living in sin all these years. How many years has it been?"

"It was 66 years in June," said Tina. "The wild roses were just beginning to bloom."

"Sixty-six years!" exclaimed Paul with a sidelong glance at Ulla. "Have you been happy all these years?"

Tina and Nils gazed fondly at each other.

"Shall we answer such a silly question, Nils?"

"Silly questions don't deserve answers," the old man replied.

"I know it's a silly question, and I already know your answer. But I want my ears to hear it said," said Paul.

"Pastor Amundson really wants *my* ears to hear it," said Ulla, darting a provoked look in his direction and kicking his leg under the table. "He forgets that happiness has as many definitions as there are people who define it. Some people who claim to be happy neglect to say that their happiness is the perverse enjoyment of inflicting pain on others."

Oblivious to the sudden dark crosscurrents, Nils and Tina pondered their response to the silly question.

Nils spoke first. "Sure we was happy! Of course we had our ups and downs now and then. What was the longest time you wouldn't talk to me, Tina?"

"Surely you haven't forgotten *that*, Nils!"

"That time Ulla's pa and I went out on the lake fishing?"

"And I begged you not to because my bones told me it was going to storm. My bones are always right, and it did storm!"

"Ya, that was a bad one! We almost didn't make it back. When we did, you cried and you laughed and you hit me and you hugged me and kissed me and you yelled at me—and then you wouldn't talk to me for a whole week."

"My bones *knew* it was going to storm. I begged you, Nils. The children hung on to you and begged you. But you were stubborn."

"Ya, I should've known better. I guess the trouble was that I couldn't knuckle under to a woman in front of Ulla's pa and let him think I was tied to my wife's apron strings."

"But I have to say one thing for you, Nils. It's always you who makes the first move to make up. You did it that time, too."

Tina squeezed Nils's hand tightly. "Do you remember the next Sunday? There was Holy Communion. We didn't have it so often in those days, and we weren't expecting it. We stood up, and the pastor stood up there at the altar and said, 'Beloved in the Lord!'

"Remember, Pastor, this was the communion service in the black hymnbook. If you want to know the truth, we old folks prefer the black hymnbook to the red and the green!

" 'Beloved in the Lord,' the pastor said, 'let us draw near with a true heart, and confess our sins unto God our Father, beseeching Him, in the name of our Lord Jesus Christ, to grant us forgiveness.' Nils and I both thought of it at once. We hadn't spoken to each other for a week! And it was you, Nils, who reached out your hand first and took my hand, and I forgave you and you forgave me and the Lord forgave us both."

"And you lived happily ever after! Please notice," said Paul, "that I did not place a question mark after that."

Tina was still remembering that most serious tiff in their lives together. "I never used the silent treatment on Nils again. It always punishes the children more than it punishes the one you are trying to punish."

"Your kids were lucky," said Ulla, her eyes brimming with tears. "Your silence lasted six days. What if it lasts six years? Six plus six plus six?"

"Ya, *stakkars!* We know!" murmured Nils, patting Ulla's hand.

"We know! We know!" whispered Tina.

There was such grief and compassion in their murmurs that Paul knew that they knew things he did not know but needed to know if ever he was to help free Ulla. *Free her from what?* He was not sure, but one thing he knew—an unfree Ulla would never allow herself to love him. However, right now he had to rescue her from the pit into which his insensitive question had thrown the conversation.

"Tina, your Princess Astrid *kringla* has made me completely forget my errand," Paul said.

He reached for his briefcase and pulled out a small packet of letters carefully wrapped in plastic and fastened with wide rubber bands. "My twin sister Maggie just returned from a year in Norway where she studied the Norwegians' work with mentally handicapped persons. During her Easter vacation she visited the farm near Stavanger where our ancestors lived. To her utter surprise the relatives there gave her this bundle of letters. All these years they have saved the letters my *oldefar* wrote to his father back in Stavanger. His mother had already died. At least a dozen letters seem to have been written from up here. The trouble is that the letters are written in Norwegian and in the old Gothic script, which may be elegant but could as well be runic writing as far as I am concerned. Can you two read this old script?"

"Shure ting! Vi can read that old-fashioned *skriving*, can't we, Tina?" In his excitement Nils lapsed into his own mixture of English and Norwegian.

He undid the bundle with shaking hands and opened the letter at the bottom of the pack. The two snowy heads bent over the letter.

"Can you read it? Is it from up here?" Nils asked.

"You can just bet your tintype it's from up here! It was written in July 1912," said Tina.

"Probably the last letter he ever wrote," whispered Paul.

"Kaerligste hilsen til dig, Far, i gamle Norge, fra din søn og svigerdatter og dit nye barnebarn i det nye land. Det er utrolig, Far, hvor meget nord-Minnesota ligner Norge!" read Tina.

"Ya, but Tina, Pastor doesn't *forstaa Norsk!*" exclaimed Nils.

Tina read the salutation again in English. "Loving greetings to you, father, in old Norway from your son in the new land and from your daughter-in-law and new grandchild. It is unbelievable, father, how much northern Minnesota is like Norway."

"See!" said Nils proudly. "Tina can read your letters okay. And she can *skrive* good, and she'll *skrive* dem out for you *paa Engelsk.*"

Tina's eyes traveled swiftly through the letter. "He sends greetings from Fru Pastor and talks about the baby and about the Bible class and about how *flink*—that means smart—the boys and girls are. That means Nils and me, too!"

"Did he write anything about your saying the books of the Bible faster than that smart Helga?" teased Paul.

"Nay! Nay! He didn't do that," laughed Tina. "That would have been silly."

"Do you mean my grandmother?" asked Ulla. "You never told me that she went to summer Bible school with you."

"She did. And I could say the books of the Bible faster than she could."

"So my *oldefar* taught your grandmother, Ulla!" Paul exclaimed. "It seems that our roots are plaited like your braid. Maybe there should be a splicing in the higher branches?" He tugged teasingly at Ulla's braid. "By the way, did *you* ever memorize the books of the Bible?"

"I did, and I challenge you to a match."

"Challenge acccpted!"

Paul handed his watch to Tina. "It's a stopwatch. You first, Ulla."

Ulla took a deep breath. Paul stopped her plunge into the recitation. "You've got an unfair advantage—the lung capacity of a long-distance runner."

"And *you* have the unfair advantage of daily hobnobbing with the Bible."

"Which is not prohibited to you, ma'am."

"Nor running to you, sir!"

She took another deep breath and began to rattle off the names, barely separating them from each other. "Genesis Exodus Leviticus Numbers Deuteronomy

Joshua Judges Ruth First'n'Second Samuel First'n'-
Second Kings First'n'Second Chronicles—"

"Fifteen seconds!" cried Tina when Ulla finished.
"Pastor, you can't beat that!"

"Here goes! Genes, Exo, Levi, Num, Deutero, Josh,
Judges, Ruth, Sam, Sam, King, King, Chron, Chron—"

"No fair! No fair!" shouted Ulla, leaping to her feet,
plunging her hands into his hair, and tugging like a
termagant, but laughing so hard that she had to sit
down.

"My friends and I worked out that scheme in Bible
school. It helped a lot at the seminary. Want to hear the
Epistles?   Rom, Cor, Cor, Gal, Ephes, Phi, Co, Thes,
Thes, Tim, Tim, Tit, Phil, Heb, James, Pet, Pet, John,
John, John, Jude, Rev—I must say that old scheme
helped me the other day in Good Harbor when that
woman tried to embarrass me. I remembered that Hab
came after Mike and before Hag."

*Ulla, Ulla, love of my life, if you could only see your face
as I see it right this moment! You have never looked so radiant
and free! But it won't last,* he thought with a pang. *It's a
happening, not a rebirth. A happy happening. But it will pass.
Oh, shut up,* he snapped at his misgivings. *Be happy that
it happened!*

Paul drove Ulla back to her parents' condominium in
Good Harbor, but she had slipped back into her shadows
again and did not invite him to come in. She stood with
her hand on the door and looked almost pleadingly into
his eyes, "Please don't try to persuade me by being so
charming! I refuse to become emotionally involved with
you or with anyone."

"You make being emotionally involved sound like a
disease, like shingles or leprosy. If it is a disease, Ulla,

then I've got it bad, and I pray that it is highly contagious."

She closed the door in his face.

Seven

Most of Wednesday was spent at Haven Home, the nursing home for the elderly in Good Harbor. It started with a telephone call that came as he was briskly towelling himself after his daily morning plunge into the frigid water of the lake. A member of his congregation there called to ask, "Pastor, is it possible for you to lead a midweek devotion at Haven Home? The retired Methodist pastor who spends his summers here in a trailer in the trailer court was going to do it, but he was called home to Iowa unexpectedly by a death in the family."

What do you say to people who have come to the end of their days? he wondered as he drove to Good Harbor. He was still wondering when he stood behind the lectern that had been pushed into the dining room for his use and faced the residents sagging in their chairs and wheelchairs, glumly looking up at him.

I don't blame them for looking glum, he thought. *They are expecting to hear the same old dulldull cliches they've heard dozens of times in these pious little "devotional hours." Why not startle them? Wake them up? Put some new wine into these old bottles?* Suddenly he was startled by the thought that perhaps *they* had something to say to *him*. Behind their empty eyes, behind the mesh of wrinkles, behind their bony or flabby or bored faces, perhaps they had a thimbleful of vintage wine *for him?*

"Are you afraid to die?" he asked bluntly, even though he knew that a resident had died the day before and knew that they knew it.

Dead silence, then shocked silence, then a peevish disquiet like the fidgets that invade a congregation when a baby fusses and is allowed to go on fussing. He let them fidget for a long minute. Their hands fretted with the cups for the midmorning coffee that would follow the devotion.

Then he abruptly left the lectern and walked among them. "Are you afraid to die?" he repeated gently. "I really want to know. You see, I'm still wet behind the ears. I'm only 27 years old. I want to know what death looks like to someone who is—how old are you?" he asked a shrunken old man strapped in a padded wheelchair. "Please tell me your name and then tell me how old you are."

"Benny Miller. I'm pushin' 85."

He went from one to one, touched them, and wondered how it must feel to grow backward, backward to complete dependence. Their glumness began to disappear, and they eagerly told him their names and ages. They had reached the age when they were no longer reluctant to tell how old they were. Indeed, some of them lied themselves older than they actually were. When he came back to Benny again, they were all sitting a little straighter in their chairs, and the dullness in their eyes, like an extra eyelid, had been raised.

61

"Well, Benny, are you ready to answer my question? Are you afraid to die?"

"Well, Pastor, I haven't exactly lived a perfect life. I got my faults. I guess I gotta admit I'm sort of scared to meet my Maker."

Bolstered by Benny's candor, a gaunt hulk of a once-giant of a man exclaimed, "I ain't scared. I'm 'shamed! I've been an ornery old cuss in my day. My kids hate my guts, and I s'pose that's why they never come to see me. I'm so ornery I cut them out of my will. Told them so, too! I'm gonna leave everything to Oral Roberts. If anyone can get me into heaven, he can."

"But we're Christians!" a feminine voice cried shrilly from the back of the room. "We don't have to be scared and ashamed! I'm not one bit afraid of dying 'cause Jesus Christ took all my sins away and washed me whiter than snow."

"I'm not afraid 'cause I read my Bible every day and say my prayers," volunteered another feminine voice.

"It don't make her any kinder to the help!" muttered Benny.

The discussion became livelier and livelier. At times it seemed a boasting contest about who among them was the greatest of sinners—or about who was the most Christian. At times it was like a tennis match with the contestants batting Bible verses back and forth at each other. Gradually the competitiveness subsided, and a different spirit slipped into the room.

"I'm not afraid," whispered a minikin of a woman. "I know the way home."

"Amazing grace!" cried another. "We've all forgotten about amazing grace!"

"Do you know who wrote the song 'Amazing Grace'?" Paul asked.

None of them knew, so he told them about John Newton, the captain of a British slave ship, who sailed down the coast of West Africa around the middle of the 18th century, bought blacks that had been captured in the jungles, chained them in the dark and sweltering hold of the ship, and then sailed to the West Indies to sell them as slaves to British plantation owners. Captain Newton then carried a shipload of plantation products to Britain, then went back down the coast of Africa to fill the ship again with slaves. Three times he made that triangular journey.

"And all the time he felt himself to be a good, pious Christian," Paul said. "He could quote Bible verses perhaps far better than you or I can. But suddenly the Holy Spirit turned a spotlight on what Captain John Newton was doing, and the captain saw the dreadfulness of his sin. He repented, quit being a captain of a slave ship, and became a preacher.

"Captain John Newton—no, excuse me, he was no longer Captain John Newton, he was preacher John Newton—preached so powerfully against slavery that he aroused the British nation, and it was the first great nation to abolish slavery. I used to think John Newton was exaggerating when he called himself a 'wretch,' but when I learned his story I knew that he truly felt himself to be a wretch. But he just as truly felt himself forgiven by God through his Son Jesus Christ. And so are you, and so am I—no matter how dark our sins, or dark our virtues! And we need not fear death, for whether we live or whether we die—perhaps die this very night— we are the Lord's!"

With that, Paul straightened his shoulders, filled his lungs with air, and sang "Amazing Grace" in a voice so powerful and exultant that it brought the kitchen help and the aides to the door to listen.

After a leisurely coffee hour with the residents who had come to the devotion, Paul visited the residents confined to their beds, talked with them about what they most wanted to talk about, then talked about that which they wanted to talk about but were too shy to do so— the life of the spirit. Trusting that they still could hear and understand, he talked and prayed with those who could not or would not talk. Even when confusion seemed to rule their minds, he stayed 10 or 15 minutes with them, even with those who could not stop their continual whimpering and moaning. When he found that singing to them seemed to quiet them, he sang them to listening silence and then prayed very simply for them.

The aide who took him into the room of the last patient he visited said, "This one is pretty far gone into senility."

Nevertheless Paul held the dried, dark claw of her hand while she babbled. "Is that you, Karl? Have you milked the cows? Did you wash their udders before you milked? You know how mad grandma gets when you don't! Did you, Karl? Answer me! Can't you talk? Has the cat got your tongue? Why don't you talk any more? You're getting just like your pa!"

"I am not Karl, but I am sure that the cows are milked," Paul said soothingly.

"Are you the doctor? Then tell them to let me out of this place. There's nothing wrong with me. I have to go home and pick the currants and make jelly."

"No, I am not the doctor. I'm Pastor Amundson, the new pastor."

The claw-fingers suddenly dug into the heel of his hand. She looked at him with terror in her eyes. "Pastor, you shouldn't have eaten those blueberries! Didn't you know that some of them were poison? Now you will die! You are going to die! Both of you are going to die!" Her voice rose to a wail, and an aide came running.

Paul drove directly from the nursing home to Dr. Lund's cabin on Half-Moon Bay and told him with unconcealed excitement about his visit with the babbling old woman.

"Obviously she confused me with my *oldefar.* Can you imagine anyone remembering something that happened 75 years ago as clearly as if it happened today?"

"Not at all surprising! Memory is like a tape. What is most recently recorded seems to deteriorate first. Preserved deep in the reel of that old woman's memory are two very lively memories. One, of your marvelous grandparents, who must have had a heap of what today we call charisma. Two, of their sudden and unexpected deaths. Something about you, Paul, stirred up those memories in that old woman."

"Her wailing about the poison berries is forever recorded on my memory reel," mused Paul. "I hope to heaven it won't haunt me forever! I didn't choose to come up here to exhume my great-grandparents' bodies, but for some strange reason, it's almost as if they are rising from the grave of their own accord."

"Why don't you ask them to lie down and rest in peace and let you come in and have some lentil soup and homemade bread with me?" Dr. Lund asked.

"That sounds better than wieners and buns in my humble home. I'll come, if you promise to go with me after supper to visit Nils and Tina and see how far along they are with translating those letters from my *oldefar* to his father in Norway."

"So you *are* interested in an exhumation of sorts, Paul."

"Only of memories, Toby. I merely want to know them better. Incidentally, *oldefar's* father in Norway would be my great-great-grandfather. I wonder what the word for that is in Norwegian?"

"If it's the same as Danish, it's a queer one—*tipoldefar*. I don't know if they keep on adding *tip* as they go back generation by generation or not."

"Tip-tip-tipoldefar!" Paul found the sound of the word so amusing that he forgot for the time being the befuddled old woman with the fraying, unraveling memory tape.

Eight

It was a marvelously soft evening. The waves were gently and rhythmically stroking the rocks in front of Nils's and Tina's cottage on Bergen Bay. In the light, northern summer night a freighter bound for Duluth was still visible. Nils met Paul and Dr. Lund at the door.

Tina struggled between rising from the table strewn with papers, coffee cups, and half-eaten sandwiches and tucking stray wisps of hair into her bun. "I haven't lifted a finger to tidy up the house all day," she said.

"Her fingers had another yob to do," chuckled Nils.

"Please don't get up," Paul said. "I do hope you haven't worked too hard on those letters! There's no hurry about them, you know."

"Nay, nay!" exclaimed Tina. "Translating your *olde-far's* letters is no job at all. It's jolly fun, for it takes us back to the olden times. We hope that you don't mind that we started with the last letters first. They're from up here and about all of us. We've finished all the letters he wrote the two summers he was up here."

"He even wrote about the confirmation class Tina and I were in," Nils added. He searched among the scattered papers. "Here 'tis. Your *oldefar* wrote it when he was teachin' summer Bible school in our little settlement back in Popple Valley. He was stayin' with Lissi and Lars Jenson. They're Ulla's *oldemor* and *oldefar*. But sit down, please sit down."

Tina once again struggled to rise from the table. "I'll go make coffee."

"Thank you, Tina," said Dr. Lund. "We just had coffee at my cabin. If I drink more, I won't sleep tonight."

"I would rather hear some of *oldefar*'s letters than have a cup of coffee," said Paul. "Please read the one you have in your hand, Nils."

Dr. Lund settled back in the rocking chair by the Jøtul wood stove, lit his pipe, and crossed his legs. Paul sat on the couch against the wall, leaning forward, his eyes intent on the letter.

"It's dated July 20, 1911," Nils began. " 'My dearest father! Loving greetings from—' But maybe we should skip the greetings at the beginning and the end. The letters we oldtimers wrote back to the old country were mostly greetings. *'Hils Far, hils Mor, hils Tante Agnes, hils Onkel John.'* Everyone had to be *hilsed!"*

"Please don't leave out anything," said Paul. "I want to hear the commas, colons, semicolons, periods, exclamation marks, question marks—everything!"

"Okay, then, here we go! 'Loving greetings from your son in America. Greetings, too, from Uncle Jørgen and Aunt Birgit and the whole family in Kandiyohi County in Minnesota. I visited them for three weeks after seminary was out and helped Uncle Jørgen with the farm work, although he seems to think that a man who is going to be a preacher should not dirty his hands. I had to remind him several times that our Lord and Savior came to be a servant to all. Uncle Jørgen is the *klokker* in the little church there, and he had me preach every Sunday because their preacher can come only once a month. He asks me to tell you that "your little laddie boy" will probably end up being a bishop. Of course he is yust yoking!' "

"Nils," interrupted Tina. "I didn't write 'yust yoking'! I wrote 'just joking.' "

"Tina, you know yolly well that I yust can't say yust and yail and yob and yump when I get excited, and I'm excited now, so you yust yump in the lake and let me go on."

Nils turned again to the letter. " 'Now I am in northern Minnesota and will be here in Yuly and August preaching and teaching summer Bible school. I feel as if I am back in Stavanger again. I came on a boat from Duluth and landed at the dock in Bergen. Ya, Bergen! Many places in Minnesota have Norwegian place names. Almost everyone up here talks Norwegian. The men farm or fish or work in the woods. The woodsmen are called—' Here we go again, Tina!—'lumberyacks.' "

"Lumberjacks, Nils," Tina corrected.

"Ya, ya! You're right, Tina. Lumberyacks it is. 'I am staying with the Jenson family while I am teaching Bible school in this little settlement. They treat me as if I were the royal family. They were even going to have me eat alone in the room that is used only for company, but I objected, and now I sit in the kitchen and eat with the family.' "

"That's Ulla's *oldefar* and *oldemor's* family," reminded Tina.

" 'The family is made up of Lars and his wife Lissi and a 16-year-old daughter, Helga, and a 14-year-old son, Erik. The children and I walk together to and from the schoolhouse where I teach Bible school and preach on Sundays.' "

"Nils and me and the neighbor children walked along with them, too," interrupted Tina, "and you can just bet that there was a lot of teasing and monkeyshines. That is, after we found out what fun Teacher was out of school. In school he was always Teacher, but out of school he was one of us."

"And you can yust bet that the girls all lost their hearts to him."

"Not me, Nils. I had already lost my heart to you."

"Ya, sure, but Helga Jenson and the others, they sure couldn't hide that they was smittin'. Your *oldefar* didn't say anything about that in this letter, but he mentioned the confirmation class. 'My confirmation class has some boys who are as tall as I am and some fully grown girls. Some, like Helga, are as smart and good-looking as any I have met in St. Paul.' "

"She *was* good-looking, Pastor," said Tina. "Ulla looks a lot like her grandmother. Helga got her looks from her father. He was what we called a 'black Norwegian.' "

"Descendants of the dark Italian and Spanish girls the Viking raiders captured and brought back to Norway," Dr. Lund muttered to Paul.

"Ya, Lars Jenson was as good as he was good-lookin', He had to be to make up for—"

"Now, Nils, no backbiting!" Tina exclaimed.

"Okay, Tina! After your *oldefar* says that about Helga he writes, 'But don't worry, Father, I'm not going to get married for at least ten years. I want to give myself fully and completely to the Lord's service before I start a family.' That's what your *oldefar* wrote in Yuly, and in September he fell in love. Like a ton of bricks, I guess, for he married in October."

"I'm surprised that he was allowed to get married when he was going to the seminary," said Paul. "They used to be pretty strict about that."

"Oh," cried Tina, "that's in one of the letters, too. They kept it a secret. He told his father, though. We haven't translated that letter yet, but we read it. That's why no one up here knew about *Fru* Pastor and the baby until they all three came up here the next summer. You see, *Fru* Pastor was a maid to a rich family in St. Paul. Your *oldefar* did odd jobs for the family to earn money to help him get through the seminary. It seems that the rich family liked your *oldefar* very much and encouraged them to get married and helped them keep it a secret."

"I guess the church officials were pretty upset when they found out," said Nils. "But the rich family had given a lot of money to the Lutheran church. Besides, Pastor was legally married, and the baby—"

"The baby came exactly nine months after the secret marriage," Tina chimed in.

"You can yust bet that they all counted! *En, to, tre*—" Nils crooked the fingers on his hands as he counted out the months.

"Some people up here were a little upset when they found out," Tina said, "but they all soon fell for *Fru* Pastor and the baby."

"Not all, Tina!" Nils exclaimed.

"Now, Nils!"

"Ya, that's water under the bridge. Well, Pastor, the rest of the letter is all greetings to people back in Stavanger. Why don't you take the letters we have finished translating, and we'll do the rest for you as soon as we can."

Paul tucked the letters they had translated into the pocket of his jacket. "I don't know how to thank you."

"Just preach a good funeral sermon for both of us," said Tina.

"That won't be hard!" Paul said. "But it's getting past your bedtime. Toby and I will—"

There was a soft knocking at the door.

"Who could that be at this time of the night?" exclaimed Tina.

It was Ulla. When she saw Paul and Dr. Lund, surprise and dismay swiftly altered her face.

"Oh, I'm sorry! I didn't know that you had guests. There wasn't a car in your driveway."

"Pastor and Dr. Lund walked over," Tina explained. "Come in, dear! Come in! Has something happened back home that makes you come so late?"

"No. I just came to say good-bye to you. I had a call today from Willmar. They are interested in having a nurse practitioner in their clinic, and they asked me to come for a job interview. It looks promising, and I may not come back for some time."

Paul and Dr. Lund had risen to their feet when she came in.

"And you weren't even going to come and say good-bye to me?" Paul asked.

"Why should I? There is nothing between us," Ulla declared.

Paul seized her by the shoulders, turned her around, and then turned both of them to face the other three. "I love this girl. I want to marry her. In the presence of you, Nils and Tina, her godparents, and you, Toby, my mentor, I ask for her hand in marriage."

Ulla jerked from his grasp and whirled to face him. "How many times do I have to tell you that I will never get married? And to you least of all. I hate you! *I hate you!*"

Her voice trailed off into sobs. She pushed him violently aside, flung open the door, and ran out into the night.

Nine

Paul followed her to the end of the public dock and stopped an elbowroom behind her. "I have you trapped," he said quietly to her back, from which all the stiffness of anger seemed to have drained. "But I won't try to stop you if you want to leave. I simply hope that we can talk honestly to each other. Not a funky honesty that wants to shock or hurt, but honesty that lets us go into the depth of ourselves to find out if we can trust each other. If we can't trust each other, why can't we? Can we talk about it, Ulla?"

She turned slowly to face him. "I have no illusions about anyone or anything. I don't believe in human attachments. Haven't I made that clear to you yet?"

"To believe that one has no illusions is an illusion in itself: the illusion that to have no illusions and no human attachments spares one pain. Is your illusionless, detached life a thing of joy, Ulla?"

"It's hell, and you know it, so don't be cruel."

"Do you trust me enough to talk about it?"

"Are you a licensed psychiatrist as well as an ordained minister?" she asked bitterly.

"Don't be cynical. It doesn't ring true."

"It's a long story," she sighed. "We had better sit down."

They dangled their feet over the edge of the dock and listened to the waves lap the pilings.

"I shall try to be as unfunkily honest as I can be," Ulla began. "But as you listen to what I have to say, please don't think that I think myself to be so different from other people, so interesting and fine and sensitive that everything and everyone else is dull and shabby and false by comparison. I distrust myself and hate myself as much as I distrust and hate most people."

"If you have been trying to hide that fact, I must say that you haven't succeeded very well."

"Please don't preach to me, Preacher man!"

"I hereby order the preacher and the teacher in me to shut up. Mind, be still! I'm all heart, Ulla."

"Don't get the illusion that this is going to be a heart-to-heart talk. I speak with my mind, not my heart! My heart is a desert and has been as long as I can remember. I suppose that's why—." She was silent for a long moment. "I suppose that's why I went to the river and the woods so early in my life and found comfort there. No child can endure a life that is all pain without finding some comfort somewhere. I found my comfort and my happiness in the river and the woods—and my family, a fox that I let out of a trap. He lost his leg, but he was still living when I went East to do graduate work. A fawn whose mother was shot out of season. I secretly bottle-fed it on milk from Grandma's Jersey cow, but a wolf got it before it could live on its own.

"I didn't try to make pets out of my friends. I would sit very still and watch them, and finally they began to accept me as a strange and harmless animal. So please don't think that I was never happy. Sometimes I was ecstatically happy, but it was always under my own solitary sun. I had no one, no human being, to share it with. I called my happiness 'bird happiness,' not human happiness, for the humans I knew weren't happy. They didn't make me bird happy. *You* do, Paul. I have to say that in all honesty. But I don't trust any happiness that I sometimes genuinely experience with some humans. I don't trust that it can survive—survive life, that is."

A childhood of solitude, nature, and books, thought Paul. *No wonder she doesn't talk like any other girl I know. A woodland poet. Emily Dickinson—with the wilderness as her Amherst.* He suddenly remembered Emily Dickinson's poem on memory, about it being like a house with a garret "for refuse and the mouse" and "the deepest cellar that ever mason hewed." It ended with the line, "Ourselves be not pursued." *Pursued! Ulla was pursued by black memories that crept out of the deepest cellar and blotted out the few happy memories she had.*

"Later I found my comfort in books," continued Ulla after a moody silence. "So then I had two happinesses— bird happiness and book happiness. Because I loved books, I loved to study, and because I loved to study, I made such a good academic record that at the university and Yale grants and fellowships just came my way. I wasn't out to get them. I wasn't trying to rank first in the class or anything like that. I simply loved books."

"Books are written by human beings, Ulla."

"Yes," she answered sharply, "but if you read the biographies and autobiographies of most authors, you learn that they had wretchedly unhappy lives and dreadful marriages. Well, to go on with my sad saga, I wasn't out to get grants and scholarships. I was only trying to ease my pain by studying hard."

"Does the pain have a name?"

"The pain of living with hatred. *Hatred!*" She almost spat the word at him. "The hatred of my family masked itself pretty much to outsiders, but within the family it was and is sheer unadulterated hatred that has lasted so long that it has become a perverse habit, a sort of perverse affection. The appalling thing is that my parents may even think that they are happy! They still sleep together, my father and mother. Can you imagine two people hating each other and still sleeping together? Sometimes I almost believe that my father had intercourse with my mother in the violence of hatred and that I was conceived in hatred. Sometimes I fear that there's a hate streak or strain that has come down through the whole family and that I have it, too, and can never rid myself of it. I could pass it on to my children, Paul. That's why I don't want children. Did you know that Loren Eiseley chose not to have children because of the madness on his mother's side of the family? Well, I seem to have a hate strain on my father's side."

Paul put his arm around her to draw her close, but she shook it off. "You would just be another comfort, Paul, not a cure. If I am tainted with hate, I can only hurt you—or anyone else with whom I form an attachment."

"There is no such thing as inherited hate. Human beings are not born to hate. They are born to love."

"Not *my* family, Paul! Somewhere and sometime way back something went wrong in my family, and mother, father, and I are caught and tangled up in it. My father and mother live in silence that screams of hate. My father grew up back there in Popple Valley on the homestead you saw on Monday. He wasn't born there, but during the Depression his parents lost their farm and moved back to the homestead and lived with my father's widowed grandmother and uncle. His father died soon after that move. My great-grandfather had died quite young, too, but great-grandmother Lissi lived until she was 80 years old. She died the year I was born, so I don't remember her. They say that she was a hard-hearted, hard-headed Tartar, given to screaming rages at her husband and her two children. My grandmother apparently feared and hated her. My great-uncle Erik did, too. Anyway, he withdrew into silence and work long before I got to know him. He became the bachelor hired hand—or slave—he wasn't paid. My father grew up there and became the second hired hand and slave. He and Erik both took their orders from women. They were more than just henpecked. If you can imagine a female bullying, you can say that the women in their lives bullied them. My father grew such a hatred of women that I wonder why he ever married. Probably to revenge himself on the female race. He dreamed of having a son. I think he wanted a boy who would grow up and be a carpenter with him. They would be 'Fjelstad and Son.' And then his only child—my parents married late in life—had to be me, a female."

"A female so lovely that the local preacher fell desperately in love with her," murmured Paul in the silence in which she caught her breath after her rush of words.

"And that male will be a desperate fool if he persists with that fatal female!"

"Love can absorb all bitterness."

"Wait with your positive aphorisms, Paul. I'm not through yet. My father was a fisherman and a part-time carpenter, and we lived a mile from here at the mouth of Rosehip Creek. When I was old enough to be conscious of my parents' hatred of each other—I'm sure my subconscious was always aware of it—when I became conscious of the cruelty of the silent meals and the long, silent evenings, I escaped to the Popple Valley homestead. It was a comfort as long as Great-uncle Erik lived. He was a big, silent man who loved his animals, his fields, and his garden. I think he loved me in the same way he loved his golden retriever Sam and the Jersey calves, Lily and Tillie. Anyway, he let me tag along with him all day long. I can still see the dark, wet patches on his bib overalls from kneeling to weed his carrots and beets. He died when I was 11, and then I began escaping to the river and the woods by day and to books by night. But I've told you all about that."

She lapsed into a long silence, broken only by the eerie call of a loon out near the point.

"If you are through with your sad story, Ulla, may I ask you a question?"

"Go ahead," she answered listlessly.

"Will you marry me?"

Her anger blazed again, and her words hit the air like hailstones in a summer storm. "Haven't you heard enough yet? Or are you such a fool that you are thinking, Poor, poor Ulla! She has no models of a good marriage. But I will marry her, and *our* marriage will be different. God and I together will help Ulla get her act together."

"Please, Ulla, I would never be guilty of that cliché."

"No, I guess you wouldn't. But you are guilty of thinking that God and you together will help me overcome all the domestic tragedies in my life. But you see, Paul, those domestic tragedies aren't just in *my* life. Look anywhere you please, and you see the corpses of marriages, whether or not the married couple divorce or stay together until death divorces them. Believe me, a lot of women—and I suppose men, too—are waiting for death to do it. If not all marriages are bad or sad, they are all drabdrabdrab."

"What about Nils and Tina?"

"I knew you would ask that. They are a rare and wonderful couple, and I admit that their life is full of grace and beauty. In their simplicity they have perfected the art of living together that fulfills both of them, but it would not fulfill me. Their life is authentic but unadventurous. No unexpecteds. They are not bored, but I would be bored with the routine sameness and orderliness of their lives. I'm afraid I would find it dreadfully monotonous. Tina and Nils cannot be my models for a happy marriage. So I have no models.

"And I'm full of fears, Paul. I grew up love-starved. I knew none of the graces of human love, and I fear that I can bring no graces to a marriage. I am afraid that I might become sick of being Mrs. Pastor, sick of being Mrs. Young Matron making peanut butter and jelly sandwiches for her kids and drinking coffee with other young mothers and discussing our problems with our kids and our husbands—and our unfulfilled lives. I'm afraid of becoming bored with you, Paul—sick of you and still having to continue to sleep with you. Romantic love is doomed, Paul! It simply can't survive marriage. Tina's and Nils's romantic love died a half century or more ago. Their marriage is just a cozy habit."

"If I were 90 years old and still had a cozy habit marriage," said Paul, "I am sure that I would thank God morning, noon, and night for making his face shine upon our marriage all the years of our life together."

She scrambled to her feet, and when he, too, stood up, she leaned so close that when he bent to her face he felt her tears against his cheek.

"I know that I have hurt you," Ulla said softly. "I know that I am hurting you now. I don't want to. Please believe that I don't want to. But since we are being unfunkily honest, I have to say the most hurtful thing of all to you. When I have said it, please let me go on my way and far, far away.

"You would not be a true pastor, Paul, if you did not draw God into everything. But your God seems to be no more capable of making wedlock holy than a fly is capable of changing the weather. My father and mother may live in frigid silence and mutual hatred at home, but they go to church every single Sunday and chant the liturgy and praise God from whom all blessings flow and go to communion and chat with people during fellowship hour afterward. My grandfather and grandmother did the same. In church every time there was church. By horses and sleigh in the winter. And my great-grandparents were charter members of St. Andrew Lutheran Church, of *your* congregation, Paul. My great-grandfather is listed as the founding father, but I'm sure that behind the scenes my great-grandmother was the real founder. If God doesn't have any more influence on souls than a fly, do you still have illusions that you can change souls? Even if I were wildly in love with you, and I'm fighting hard not to be, I could never join such a feeble alliance as God and Pastor Paul."

Paul silently watched her walk resolutely down the dock, called to her only when she reached the shore. "Ulla, just one question!"

"Make it short!"

"Will you marry me?"

A loon laughed its maniacal, demented laugh, and he knew it was Ulla's perfect imitation and not one of the pair of loons that claimed Bergen Bay as their exclusive territory.

Ten

"Is it too late, Doctor?" Paul asked when Dr. Lund opened the door to his soft knock half an hour later. "Are you on all-night emergency duty tonight, ready and willing to bind up any and all wounds and fractures? Even wounded love and broken hearts?"

"Never too late for you, Paul. Come in! But you don't seem to be in shock, and I don't see any blood. I even heard you whistle as you came down the path. Did true love win a victory? If so, it bears out what Thomas Hardy said in *Far from the Madding Crowd:* 'The more emphatic the renunciation, the less absolute its character.' "

"Oh, the renunciation was absolute, all right. True love bit the dust, but I don't eat dust. I whistle because I don't believe in defeat."

Paul sat down on the Swedish-blue couch. His eyes surveyed the room lit only by three candles in a three-branched candelabrum. A blue teapot and two matching cups sat on the coffee table.

"It looks as if you were expecting me," Paul said.

"I gave up expectations long ago. That makes every-thing that happens unexpected. More fun that way."

"How do you explain two teacups, then?"

"Beth and I always had a cup of herbal tea before we went to bed, and I always set a cup for her. She seems closest at this hour of the night. And the Swede in me loves candlelight. Do you know that I counted 450 can-dles in my village church in Sweden last Christmas? It was beautiful, but it's a wonder we didn't all suffocate with all those candles burning up the oxygen. I love candlelight, and I am not one who lights the candles when I hear the invited guests at the door and blows them out as soon as I shut the door on their departure. But that doesn't mean that I'm a romantic, Paul. I don't happen to believe that love conquers all. To be bluntly honest, I believe that Ulla has been so damaged by life-long mental abuse that she can never love and trust anyone. Her wounds are deep and permanent, I'm afraid. Don't expect a miracle, Paul."

"I gave up expectations long ago, Toby," said Paul, a mischievous twinkle in his eyes, "but I don't rule out the unexpected. Or miracles. By the rigid laws of the mind, Ulla's psyche may be permanently damaged. I happen to believe that the Divine Synthesizer created us a synthesis of mind, body, and spirit, and I choose to believe and live in the wonder-working freedom of the spirit. His Holiness, the Lord of the Spirit, excels in the unexpected, and he finds cracks in the most im-pregnable mental blockades.

"You are absolutely right, Toby, I am quite unable to storm Ulla's fortress and overwhelm her with my human love. Or to perform a miraculous healing of the mem-ories that haunt and pursue her. I have no confidence in myself, but I have every confidence in the Holy Spirit. Thanks be to him—or to her, if you insist—I believe in possibility, the possibility of human transformation. I refuse to accept bad news, or bad pasts. The Greeks thought it was impossible to alter the past. One of their aphorisms said that even the gods cannot alter the past. But our God can. Why else did Jesus tell the parable of the prodigal son? The father's continuous love, the son's repentance, and the father's forgiveness altered the prodigal son's bad past. Ulla is the victim of a bad past, more sinned against than sinning, but I have unshakable faith that Christ can perform the miracle that I cannot do."

"That explains why you can come whistling from Ulla's rather violent rejection of your proposal of marriage. Well, if you don't want advice and counseling from the Sage of the North Shore, what do you want?"

"I want to understand how it happened that such a wonderful and intelligent girl as Ulla has closed the door to human relationships. She told me enough just now so that I understand why it happened, but *how* did it happen. Can you tell me more about her family?"

"After you and Ulla left so abruptly and dramatically tonight, Nils and Tina added considerably to the bits and pieces of that family tragedy I have learned and surmised over the years. Did you know that the confused old woman you visited today at Haven Home, the one who babbled about the poison berries, is Ulla's grandmother?"

"The one who cried, 'Pastor, you shouldn't have eaten those berries?' *She* is Ulla's grandmother?"

"She is Helga Jenson, the 16-year-old girl in the family with whom your great-grandfather lived when he was a summer Bible school teacher and preacher up here, Tina's rival when it came to saying the books of the Bible the fastest."

"So that poor woman in the nursing home at Good Harbor is part of Ulla's tragic story!" Paul exclaimed.

"According to Nils, it was Helga's mother, Lissi, who held the whip in the family. Tina said she wore her hair done up tight and looked very godly, like a missionary. Nils said she may have looked godly, but she had an ungodly temperament and a will of cast iron. He called her a *gammel hex*, which I think means an old witch. Tina, of course, scolded him and reminded him of the Eighth Commandment—in fact, recited Luther's whole explanation of it in Norwegian. What a memory that woman has!"

"While Ulla's grandmother Helga lies there in Haven Home with no memory at all!" Paul added.

"No memory? She hasn't forgotten your great-grandparents' deaths from eating poison berries! Incidentally, have *you* forgotten your great-grandfather's letters to his father in Norway?"

"Holy smoke, yes!" Paul fumbled in his jacket pocket and drew out the small packet of translated letters. "These are the letters he wrote from up here. Of course I'm most interested in the very last letter he wrote. Hey, how about a better light?"

"Let's hear it," said Dr. Lund, turning on the table lamp. "Let me have the original. You read Nils's and Tina's translation, and I'll try to follow along. The Gothic script can't be much worse than a physician's prescription. I've written thousands of them in my lifetime. As for the language, I know a little Swedish after last year, and it's a lot like Norwegian."

"*Oldefar* dates this letter July 1912," Paul began. "Apparently he didn't write the whole letter at one time. Probably began it early in the month and finished and mailed it toward the end of the month.

" 'My dearest father,' " Paul read. " 'Loving greetings to you, father, in old Norway, from your son in the new land and from your daughter-in-law and your new grandson. It is unbelievable, father, how much northern Minnesota is like Norway! We have fjords (Lake Superior), mountains (the highest hills in Minnesota), mountain rivers, forests of birch and evergreen. I have written all this before, but I never cease to wonder at the resemblance. We feel very much at home here.' Are you able to follow the letter, Toby?" Paul asked.

"Shure ting, as Nils says. I'm recognizing the key words, at least. Go on!"

" 'But our greatest joy, of course, is not nature but the precious new life that God has given us. Mikkel looks like you, father, but he has Maggie's lovely red hair. He is a month old now and already smiles and coos. Maggie says he coos in Irish, but I say he coos in Norwegian. We take him with us everywhere we go—even berry picking. Many of the same berries grow wild here that grow in Norway—strawberries, currants, cherries, blueberries, raspberries. Maggie has already made wild strawberry and wild raspberry preserves. My pastoral work is going very well. I am preparing the confirmation class I started last year for confirmation this fall. They will be ready for it, for they know their Bible and Luther's Catechism very well and are strong in the faith.' "

"Wait a minute!" interrupted Dr. Lund. "Nils's and Tina's translation seems to have left out something. I followed you through wild strawberry and raspberry preserves, but I lost you there."

"Do you find 'My pastoral work is going very well'?"

"Hmmm—let's see—yes, a few lines down the paper. *'Min pastoral arbeid—'* Tina seems to have skipped a few lines."

"Strange! She's so very meticulous. Can you make out anything that she left out?"

"I'm slowly getting the hang of the Gothic script. I'll fetch my Swedish-English dictionary, and we'll make a stab at it."

"It's pretty late. We could wait until tomorrow and take the letter back to Tina and Nils."

"Tina gets a feeling in her bones when a storm is brewing. The neurons in my brain begin to quiver when something is—"

"Is what, Toby?"

"Is very wrong! Here's a pencil and a sheet of paper. I'll try to translate, and you write it down."

Dr. Lund slid his sagging bifocals up his nose and bent over the letter. "The first word is easy. *Snart*—soon. Blueberries is a cinch. The words in between—Heck, I don't need a dictionary! *Vi vil plukke.* Pluck! Soon we will be plucking blueberries. Next sentence—the word blueberry again, but this time it's two separate words—blue berry.

" 'There is a blue berry here that does not grow in Norway.' Got that down? The key word in the next sentence seems to be spelled g-i-f-t-i-g. My neurons are jumping and screaming what it means, but I'll look it up just to be sure. Yes, my neurons are right. *Poisonous.* 'It is a very poisonous berry.' "

"He knew! Oldefar *knew* that poisonous berry!" whispered Paul.

"There's one more sentence to the part Tina and Nils

left out. *'Frygt ikke, Far!'* Easy! I heard that in the Christmas Gospel in Sweden last year. It's what the angel said to the shepherds. 'Fear not!' 'Do not fear, Father. This— poisonous—blue berry—grows on a—very—' I'll look up this word just to be sure. Of course, it means *different*. 'grows—on a very different—plant—than the blueberry. We—will not—*forveklse*—dictionary says *mistake*. 'We will not mistake it.' "

The two men sat and looked at each other in silence.

"Are you sure, Toby? Are you sure that your translation is right?"

"Read it back to me, and I'll follow the original again," Dr. Lund said eagerly.

" 'Soon we will be picking blueberries. There is a blue berry here that does not grow in Norway. It is a very poisonous berry. Do not fear, father. This poisonous blue berry grows on a very different plant than the blueberry. We will not mistake it.' "

"My God, Paul! Do you know what this means?" Dr. Lund exclaimed.

"It means that my great-grandparents' deaths were not accidental! It means that someone else must have picked the poison blue berries and mixed them with the blueberries they picked and ate. But who, Toby?"

Paul went to the window and looked out at the lake. Pulses of light rose in the night sky, wavered, floated, receded, and rose again. He looked at them with unseeing eyes.

Suddenly he turned. "Why did Tina and Nils leave that part out?" he asked savagely.

"Surely you are not suspecting *them?* I'm guessing that this news surprised them as much as it did us. I'm also guessing that they have pretty good reasons for not opening up a vipers' tangle. Have you ever come upon a tangle of snakes coming out of winter's hibernation?"

"If my great-grandparents were murdered, I'm going to find out who did it, and when I find out, I'll tell the world about it," said Paul harshly. "They've had to wait 74 years for justice, but justice they shall have! Tomorrow I'm going to Nils and Tina and ask them whom they are trying to protect."

"What if they are trying to protect *you?*"

"Me?"

"Yes, *you!*"

"I don't get it!"

"Perhaps Tina and Nils don't want you to—get it."

Paul's shoulders sagged wearily. "I'm tired, confused, sad, mad. I think I'll go home."

He stopped at the door and turned around with an ironical smile. "It's pretty much to have my proposal of marriage be violently rejected and to uncover pretty strong evidence that my great-grandparents were murdered, all on the same evening!"

"Do you remember what you said to me just about an hour ago? About whistling?" Dr. Lund asked.

"I whistle because I don't accept defeat."

Dr. Lund stood in the doorway until he heard from far down his long driveway a cheerful whistling. He smiled and went back into the cabin. *I'll bet the green hymnbook left out that good old hymn Paul is whistling*, he thought. He took the black, the red, and the green hymnbooks from the shelf and searched their respective indexes. "Just as I thought! The black and the red have it. The green doesn't. It's 438 in the black. Remember it, Beth?" He sang softly:

"Come, ye disconsolate, where'er ye languish;
Come to the mercy-seat, fervently kneel;
Here bring your wounded hearts, here tell your anguish;
Earth has no sorrow that heaven cannot heal."

Eleven

Paul's daily morning routine was to leap out of bed, grab a towel, run down the path to the end of the point, fling off his pajamas, and leap feet-first off his private dock into the lake. Two minutes in the frigid water was enough. Then back to the log cabin, a brisk rubdown, after which he swiftly dressed, singing a favorite hymn lustily all the while. Then he prayed Luther's morning prayer, made the sign of the cross, committed himself and the day to the Lord, and proceeded to the first work of the day, which was to ponder the scripture texts for the next Sunday's sermon, read, and jot down notes. After an hour of that, breakfast, and then out into his two parishes to seek out those who needed the blessings the gospel has to give—or to seek out those who did not know that they needed the blessings the gospel has to give.

Luther, he had long since decided, had the right formula. Pray simply, directly, briefly. Commit one's whole self to the Lord this day and then go to work joyfully.

At night pray the evening prayer of gratitude and praise, ask for forgiveness for any sin or wrong done that day, and then lie down and go to sleep peacefully. No self-lacerations, no moaning and groaning at night. No funky-heartedness in the morning. *Carpe diem!* Seize the day the Lord has given!

But his ordinary routine had had no blessing for him last evening, and it had none this morning. It was Thursday, and Sunday's sermon should be falling into shape, but it was merely falling into the all-too-familiar pattern of pious platitudes. He wrestled with the Gospel text for a half hour. It was the story of the good Samaritan, a story that had been masticated so many times that all the delectables had been chewed out of it.

He finally gave up and went out to the point, where the lake sparkled as far as his eyes could see, and the sun drew fragrance from the cedars. But the beauty and the fragrance that had never failed to make his heart sing now failed him entirely. His eyes did not focus on the beauty, but on two visions that had tormented him most of the night. One was the vision of the death agony of his great-grandparents, poisoned by some unknown person. Who? Who could have hated that luminous constellation, Pastor Poul and his Irish bride? The other was the image of Ulla, whose taste of her self had been as effectually poisoned as had his great-grandparents' lives. What would happen to her if the poison that made her self-taste loathsome was never drawn out?

The two loons that claimed Bergen Bay for their own were swimming on the far side of the cove with their young ones. *How do they feel about themselves,* he wondered, *they who have no capacity to selve into a consciousness of self-being? What was the consciousness of self but the capacity to be wounded, poisoned? Where else but in self-loathing did self-feeling end? Lucky loons! Unhappy humans! The cap-stone of creation, yet so harassed with festering lesions!*

The sound of a car pulling into the driveway made him turn. It was Henna, Ulla's bright-orange Toyota pickup! It did not stop at the cabin door, where the driveway ended, but ploughed through the sand and wave-rounded pebbles and stones of the beach and skidded to a stop directly in front of him. He leaped to open the door, and Ulla flung her arms around his neck in a strangling embrace.

"Hold me tight!" she gasped.

He lifted her clear of the car and held her close.

"Tighter!"

"If I hold you any tighter, I'll crack your ribs. Has something terrible happened?" he asked anxiously.

"Kiss me!"

Her lips clung to his vehemently and parted only to ask, just as vehemently, "Will you marry me? For ever and ever and ever and ever? Until death does us part?"

He swung her up into his arms and kissed his answer, kissed her until the frenzy in her relaxed into a deep quietness. He carried her to the redwood beach chair near the redwood picnic table and eased into it. She snuggled against his chest and sighed contentedly.

"I am so tired, so tired! But I'm not confused anymore, Paul. I'm disburdened, light as a bird, levitated! Hang on to me, or I'll float into the wild blue yonder. I'm—oh, how I do love you, Paul! And not just you only. I want to love everyone alive. Everyone! And I'm as sure as sure can be that our marriage will not be bad, sad, or drab. I know for sure that we won't settle down like cabbages. I know for sure that our marriage will be blessed and that we will live happily ever after."

She pressed her face against him, and he felt her tears. "Amen!" he whispered.

Much later he asked quietly, "What disburdened you? In my mind I had you half way to Willmar and all the way out of my life. What happened?"

She sat up, propped her elbows on his chest, her chin on her cupped hands. Her eyes looked at him steadily. "A Lazarus miracle. An Ulla-raised-from-the-dead miracle. You *do* believe in miracles, don't you?"

"The split second after I wake up they begin happening. A little behind time this morning, but I suppose that's because this one is absolutely the most amazing, the most marvelous miracle that has ever happened in my life."

"You believe in miracles, and you've made me believe in miracles. I suppose that's why I'm not scared of my irrational fears and angers and guilts any more. I'm sure that some of them will return at times and haunt me, but I'm also dead sure that by the same miracle that happened this morning they will vanish."

She nestled her head on his shoulder and nuzzled his ear. "Do you want to hear what happened after I left you on the dock last night, after I said those horrible, hurtful things to you?"

"The ear you are nibbling on is tensing and tilting like a dog's to hear what happened to you."

"We have to have a dog, Paul! My parents would never let me have one."

"We'll have two if you want them! But what happened?"

"I drove back to Good Harbor, hating myself so violently that I almost wished that I wouldn't make the curve around Morton's Cliff. I was driving 80 in a 25-mile-an-hour zone. My parents were still up watching

TV, and for some reason—I don't know why, for I am not in the habit of sharing intimacies with them, I think it was a kind of wild despair—anyhow, I told them that you had proposed marriage and that I had refused. They were furious with me for depriving them of a preacher son-in-law. You do know, don't you, that every Lutheran parent, or at least every Lutheran mother, lusts to have her daughter marry a preacher. My grandmother once told me that her mother was dead set on having her marry your great-grandfather, and that was why she tried to move heaven and earth and perhaps hell, too, and church headquarters and the congregations in Good Harbor and Bergen to have him called up here as a pastor."

Paul's arms tightened around her. God in heaven, no! In his sudden joy he had utterly forgotten about his great-grandparents and the question that burned in his mind: Who? Who had hated them enough to poison them? And now this woman he loved was in all innocence murmuring in his ear a possible clue, a horrifying clue that pointed its finger at her own ancestor! *Lord, Lord, spare us this!* He forced his voice to be calm. "How did she feel when my great-grandfather showed up with an Irish bride and a baby?"

"Grandmother said she was sweet as apple pie to them—those were her words. But she never forgave grandma for failing to catch your great-grandfather. She never forgave the farmer my grandmother married for not being the preacher son-in-law she had hoped to get.

"Well, that's another story. My parents were furious with me when I told them that I had refused you. We quarreled. They quarreled. It was ugly and awful, and I decided to shed them and leave home forever. I decided to wipe out my whole hateful past. I emptied the closet and all my drawers, burned my diaries, letters, mementos, stripped the bed, took a bath, washed my hair, washed the floor. I literally washed myself out of the house and their lives and set out to make a completely new life for myself. I even thought of changing my name to Katie Caldwel."

"Katie is a good name for a tempestuous shrew."

"Now you're laughing at me! The sun was coming up when I was finally all packed up and ready to leave. Did you see the sunrise this morning, Paul?"

"I was riding nightmares, Ulla."

"Because of me," she said ruefully. "It was the most beautiful sunrise I have ever seen! It tinted everything with glory—the lake, the sailboats in the harbor, the old lighthouse. Glory everywhere—except inside of me. There it was all deepest, darkest, blackest night."

Her arms tightened around his neck. "Kiss me!"

"I wonder if I will ever get enough of hugging and kissing," she sighed later. "Were you hugged and kissed when you were a child? Silly question! Of course you were! I can't remember ever being kissed in my family— or ever seeing anyone in my family being kissed or kissing. If we have a family, Paul, it's going to be the huggingest, kissingest family in the world."

"Verily, verily!"

"Let's name our first girl Verily!"

"If we have quadruplets, we most certainly will not give them the names an author gave to the Jersey cows on Cold Comfort Farm: Graceless, Pointless, Feckless, and Aimless."

"Cold Comfort Farm! What a fitting name for the homestead in Popple Valley! There was a Jersey cow down on my grandparents' farm," murmured Ulla sleepily.

"Hey, now! You musn't go to sleep until you have told me the miracle!"

Ulla sat bolt upright in his lap. "Your face was on every billboard and signboard all the way to Duluth. The highway signs didn't say 'So-and-so many miles to Duluth.' Your face was on them, and you said, 'Ulla, I am so-and-so many miles behind you and getting farther away every minute.' You were in the Ford Tempo on the billboard, 'The Forward-Thinking Car!' You looked straight at me and said, 'Ulla, life is lived forward, not backward.' "

"If you had seen Søren Kierkegaard's face on the billboard he would have said, 'Life is lived forward and understood backward.' "

"I didn't see Søren's face anywhere, but finally I began seeing you on every bush and every tree. I was terribly, dangerously tired, so I stopped at the rest stop this side of Duluth and decided to sit at a picnic table, lay my head on my arms, and sleep for half an hour. That's when the miracle happened."

"Did you fall asleep and dream?"

"No, I never did fall asleep. After it happened I didn't need to sleep. And it wasn't a vision—like your face— I was seeing. It was like a—No, not *like* a—! It *was!* It was a sudden soul bath, a soul cleansing, a soul sauna. Or it was my heart that was cleansed. What a mystery they are, the soul and the heart! The cleansing agent was a shower of light. What happened was not a lavation, but a lustration. Is there such a word, Paul?"

"If there isn't, there is now."

"The light shower rinsed out every doubt, every distrust, every bitterness in my being and flooded it with light and love and trust—and such a sense of elation as

I have ever known. I laughed out loud. A middle-aged woman coming out of the restroom looked at me as if I were crazy. I jumped up, jumped into Henna, and here I am!"

"By the grace of God, here you are!" he said humbly. *And by the grace of God,* he thought, *this is a rebirth, not just a happening.*

"Yes, I suppose it is by the grace of God—the God I cruelly told you last night has no more influence on the soul than a fly. Do you forgive me?"

"The forgiveness of the forgiven-in-Christ is prevenient."

"You will have to teach me theology," she murmured sleepily, "and I'll take care of your corns and bunions and hangnails."

He felt every curve of her body relaxing completely into his own.

"Paul," she murmured soberly, "I know everything isn't always going to be straight and tidy forevermore, but I do trust and believe that living ordinary life with you will be ex—tra—ord—in—arrr—"

Her voice trailed off into silence. When he was quite sure that she was sound asleep, he carried her into the cabin and laid her on his bed. A knocking brought him swiftly to the door. It was Dr. Lund.

"Shh! She's sleeping!" Paul whispered.

"Who?"

"My true love. My soon-to-be-bride."

Twelve

It took Paul and Dr. Lund an hour to work Henna off the beach and back onto the firm driveway.

"I didn't realize that it would be so difficult," said Paul when they had succeeded in inching her out by creating a precarious *terra firma* under her wheels with planks and evergreen branches. "Being stuck in mud may not be as clean as being stuck in beach sand and sleeky pebbles and stones, but mud at least is genuinely unwilling to let go. Beach sand is a deceiving compound of willingness and unwillingness. I guess I prefer my adversary to be straightforward and not devious."

They had not spoken of Ulla as they worked, but over a thermos of coffee at the picnic table Paul announced that he had lost his urge to unravel the riddle of his great-grandparents' deaths.

"I'm afraid I'll unravel more than I wish to unravel," he said frankly. "Of course I'm thinking of Ulla, and so, I'm quite sure now, were Tina and Nils when they left out those significant lines in *Oldefar's* last letter."

"I understand you completely, my dear Holmes," said Dr. Lund, "but would you mind if your subordinate Watson carries on the investigation?"

"You would never be satisfied being Watson and playing second-fiddle sleuthhound," chuckled Paul. "Why don't you take the Sherlock Holmes role in this mystery? All I ask is that for Ulla's sake whatever you sniff out be kept forever secret. Incidentally, she innocently provided what may be a clue—at least a motive."

Dr. Lund did not seem at all surprised to hear about Lissi Jenson's bitterly frustrated hope to have her daughter Helga marry the seminary student who had roomed and boarded with them while he taught summer Bible school. "There is no question in my mind that she poisoned your great-grandparents," he said. "According to Nils and Tina—you see, I've already been to see them this morning—according to them, your great-grandparents were invited to the Jenson farm on the last day of their lives to go blueberry picking in a patch Lissi considered her own private possession. Helga and Erik went with them to the blueberry patch, and Lissi, like the good soul she wanted them to think she was, stayed home to take care of the baby and prepare lunch for them before they drove back to Good Harbor in their buggy.

"They took sick on the way and became violently ill when they arrived in Good Harbor. Lissi told everyone that they had insisted that she serve them some of their very own berries, and rather than make a fuss about it, she fixed them two big bowls of blueberries they themselves had just picked and mixed them with thick rich cream from her Jersey cow. She sent the rest of the berries they had picked home with them, plus Helga's and Erik's pails of berries. Your great-grandparents' berries did indeed prove to have poison berries in among the blueberries. But I don't think the blue-bead lily berries were enough to cause their deaths. There had to be something else, and I aim to find out what it was."

Paul listened with increasing dismay. "If all this is true, can we swear Nils and Tina to secrecy?"

"Why else do you think they deliberately left out part of your great-grandfather's letter? Moreover, it may not have been a complete surprise to them after all. They very likely have had their suspicions for almost 75 years. If you want the worst, Paul, if your mind can take foul suspicions from double or triple barrels, Nils and Tina now suspect that Lissi also poisoned her husband and Helga's husband as well. Slow poisoning in each case. The two men died too young for the sturdy Norwegian stock that settled up here on the Shore. I checked their tombstones. Lissi's husband was 45 and Helga's, 42. Nils said they both died of chronic *mavekatarr.* In those days they called almost every stomach or intestinal disorder they couldn't explain "catarrh." He said Helga's husband often complained to him of stomach pains and cramps. Tina said it would probably be called stomach ulcers now. Nils said any man who lived with that woman would have developed ulcers. But I'm pretty sure that that evil woman gave them something poisonous in small doses over a period of time. Not poison berries. Something else, and I think I know what."

Paul pushed his coffee cup aside so violently that it tipped and spilled. "Either you have a diabolical imagination, or—"

"Or what, Paul?"

"Toby, I beg you to stop looking for skeletons in Ulla's family closet! We have to protect her!"

"As if I wouldn't! As if I haven't been protecting people all my life! Protected a little three-year-old tyke who accidentally and in all innocence killed his baby sister from growing up to feel like a murderer by conspiring with his parents to attribute the death to a fall from a high chair. Protected a 16-year-old girl from what used to be a sin that branded a girl for life by sending her off to another state—to my saintly sister, as a matter of fact. With the young mother's consent gave the baby to a wonderful childless couple.

"Don't worry, Paul. You aren't the only person in the world who loves Ulla. Tina, Nils, and I don't need to swear on a stack of Bibles to protect her. Incidentally, she has waked up. I just saw her looking out the window. Wipe that tragic look off your face, or you yourself will betray her family's dark secrets!"

What would she be like after her sleep? Paul wondered as he rose to meet her. *Was there a manic-depressive streak in her family, and the manic side of the cycle had suddenly manifested itself in her? Would she now plunge back into the depression cycle?*

Oh, you of little faith, he upbraided himself as she came into his arms and lifted a radiant face for his kiss. Her skin glowed as if transilluminated, and the light within her was burning even brighter than before.

She slipped from his arms and reached both her hands to Dr. Lund. "Was it you who helped liberate Henna?"

"Just another one of the thousand or so deliveries I have made in my career," he said, kissing her on both cheeks. "At the time it wasn't particularly a pleasure, but with the arrival of Henna's enchanting owner the whole experience has turned into pure delight."

"How I wish that you weren't retired!" she exclaimed impetuously. "You are a shameless flatterer, but it would be fun to practice my profession with you. Do you have any clout with Dr. Jordan in Good Harbor? He's an excellent physician, but he's getting old. I think he needs the help of a nurse practitioner fresh out of the Yale Graduate School of Nursing."

"How do you know that your husband will let you practice your profession?" he teased. "How do you know that he won't hold his woman to the three traditional *K*s: *Kirche, Küche, und Kinder*—church, kitchen, and children?"

"Why do you suppose I came back?" she asked soberly. "Because Paul is the freest person I have ever known. Because he surrounds me with freedom. Because for the first time in my life I can breathe freely and deeply. The traditional *K*s don't scare me at all! I shall merely add one more—of my own free will! Career! Church, kitchen, kids, and career! And not one *K* will suffer neglect, I assure you!"

"Hear! Hear!" cried Paul.

"You don't deserve her," grumbled Dr. Lund.

"What are your plans for today?" Ulla asked suddenly, turning to Paul.

"Don't you think Paul has already accomplished enough for one day?" asked Dr. Lund. "The engagement to you and the disengagement of Henna?"

"My plans always yield to the unplanned," said Paul. He picked Ulla up and set her on the picnic table. "Today you are my day, Ulla, my day of days."

"For me it feels like the first day of my life. Come one, come all!" Ulla called to the sea gulls scouting the skies. "Come, celebrate the first day of my life! Do you have any stale bread, Paul?"

"Stale? Betrothal feasts should have the freshest of fresh. It so happens that yesterday two sweet parishioners left homebaked rolls and loaves on my kitchen table."

The gulls swiftly formed a clamoring ring around Ulla's head, swooping to catch the chunks of bread she laughingly tossed to them.

"Come!" she cried to other gulls soaring in from more distant points. "Come celebrate the first day of my life!"

She was breathing deeply, and her cheeks glowed redwine-red when the last gull had snatched the last chunk of bread and flown off.

"Catch me!" she cried, and jumped from the table into Paul's arms.

"If you will pardon the intrusion," said Dr. Lund at last, interrupting their embrace, "I will politely bow out now and leave you two alone to celebrate the first day of your lives."

"Oh, no!" they both exclaimed in dismay.

"You are part of the celebration, Toby," said Ulla. "When I asked Paul about his plans, I was wondering if the three of us could go back to the old homestead. Paul already knows how I feel about that place and unknowingly gave me a name for it—Cold Comfort Farm. Actually, I want to pinch the miracle that happened to me this morning. I want to test it against the dark memories I have of that place. I have to find out if the Light can chase *that* darkness away. Don't be afraid, Toby. We won't embarrass you and make it an amorous tryst. For me it will be a cold-blooded experiment. Please do come with us!"

Dr. Lund shot a significant look at Paul over Ulla's head. "I wasn't embarrassed. Merely jealous. I accept the invitation. The Sherlock Holmes in me has always been intrigued with old abandoned houses and barns."

The half-mile square of old homestead had completely surrendered its losing battle with balsam fir, poplar saplings, alder brush, skunk cabbage, and bracken. Two runty apple trees and some scraggly currant bushes were all that remained of an attempt at orchard and garden.

"My Light is already beginning to send me messages," said Ulla as they neared the end of the faint traces of the old driveway.

"Good ones, I hope," said Paul, who had been uncharacteristically silent all the way from the Shore because he was fervently praying that Ulla's Light would survive this test of darkness.

"Of course they're good!" Ulla replied. "Well, perhaps not good. Sad. Very sad. But at least they are explaining things to me that I had not thought of before. For example, the cruel loneliness of these remote farms. It's a wonder that more pioneers did not become mad as a coot! And the sunrise-to-sundown body-breaking work! And then to lose out in the end to the short growing season, the stones, and the forest.

"Just look at what has happened to my great-grandparents' vision of plowed fields and a herd of grazing Jerseys!" she said, stopping and dramatically encompassing the old homestead with a wave of her hand. "No wonder my great-grandmother turned into a bitch. Or a witch. What's the difference between a bitch and a witch?"

"A bitch bitches and a witch takes a hellish delight in being malignant and malevolent," said Dr. Lund.

"Well, then she was both. A bitch-witch. And because of her and the loneliness and the unrelieved drudgery and the futility of it all, it's no wonder Grandma Helga and my father withdrew into bitterness and silence. Suddenly everything is beginning to fit into a pattern for me. Oh, Paul!" she cried, clutching his arms. "Can psyches begun as traumatically as mine ever be rescued?"

"I've got my arms around a rescued psyche right now. In fact, I'm going to pinch that rescued psyche to convince it that its rescue is for real."

"Ouch!" she cried. "I'm a believer! A true believer! But," she added wistfully, "please help my unbelief. Will you go with me later today—first to grandmother at Haven Home, and then to my parents?"

"Listen, you two," said Dr. Lund. "Why don't you take off to Trout River gorge and go swimming? Leave me here to putter around in these interesting ruins. I might even find some square nails for my antique collection, or blue Ball Mason jars in the basement. They're worth money now."

"Don't be disappointed," said Ulla. "Vandals pulled them off the shelves and smashed them to bits. Watch out for broken glass."

When after two hours Paul and Ulla wandered back in a mellow daze of happiness, Ulla chose not to enter the house but excused herself to go behind the half-grown balsam growing out of the wreck of the outhouse.

"My bladder is bursting!" she exclaimed.

"Do you know that the famous Danish astronomer Tycho Brahe died of a burst bladder?" Dr. Lund called after her. "He was at a banquet in his honor, and in those days one did not make one's bodily needs public knowledge."

"I found what I expected and hoped to find," Dr. Lund whispered to Paul. "This tight little jar of tiny seeds was behind some jars of canned rhubarb on a moldy shelf in the dark hole in the ground the pioneers called the fruit cellar. The only jars the vandals missed. If I'm right these are the seeds of the water hemlock and are deadly poison. Very small and inconspicuous, as you see. The plant grows here and is related to the plant that produced the poison that killed Socrates."

"Toby, if you as much as breathe one word about poison to Ulla, I'll—I'll—" hissed Paul.

"Too bad we aren't Catholic," chuckled Toby. "You could excommunicate me."

"Ulla, no need to ask you if your Light dispelled the darkness of Cold Comfort Farm," said Dr. Lund to her later as they hiked back to the road where he had left his car. "I think you would glow in the dark like phosphorescence."

"Nothing in all the world," she said, dancing along between them like a child, her black braid bouncing, "nothing will ever put it out!"

Thirteen

The subject of the wedding came up on the way back to the Shore when they had to stop for a grouse mother who imperiously stood in the middle of the road and clucked her chicks, one by one, safely across the road. "Now there's a woman after my own heart," chuckled Dr. Lund. "She simply wills what has to be done and does it. No paralyzing self-reflection. Shall I or shall I not challenge this monster? Shall I call a committee meeting? Organize a demonstration? Shall we vote on the problem? Just look at her! By sheer force of will she alone stops us dead in our tracks."

"Bravo, bravo, Sister Grouse!" Ulla called, leaning out the open car window.

"Which leads me directly into a problem facing us," said Paul, "and I'm wondering, Ulla, if you will show the same force of will and pluck against this monster that your Sister Grouse just did."

"Show me the monster and watch me ruffle my feathers and boldly challenge it!"

"Church weddings."

"Church weddings!" Dr. Lund shouted with laughter, pulled the car to the side of the road, and turned off the motor. "Go to it! I've waited a long time to see that monster challenged."

"Do you mean that you two men don't believe in weddings in churches?" asked Ulla. "Do you perhaps recommend that the bridal pair make their vows in their favorite milieu? Runners at the Duluth end of Grandma's Marathon? Skiers at the top of Lutsen's ski jump? Scuba divers at the bottom of Lake Superior? Maybe standing on the wreck of the ship *The America* near Isle Royal? Sky divers floating in the clouds? Should you and I be married at the gorge on Trout River, Paul? In bathing suits?"

"Or without," said Dr. Lund. "I've heard of nudist weddings."

"Is that what you want, Paul?" asked Ulla, her cheeks flaming with anger.

"I wouldn't mind letting you think so a while longer," said Paul. "You are so beautiful when you are angry, Ulla. No, of course I don't want a farcical wedding! But that's exactly what many church weddings have become—farcy."

"Wrong word, Paul!" interrupted Dr. Lund. "Farcy is a veterinarian term—a disease affecting the superficial lymphatics and the skin of horses and mules."

"Maybe not as wrong a word as you think, Toby," said Paul. "At least an excessive superficiality has diseased the thoughts and actions of people who plan weddings. A disease primarily afflicting the mothers of brides. They seem to be most guilty of turning church weddings into pageantry."

"A promenade of penguins and peacocks!" giggled Ulla, relaxing into full agreement.

"A fashion show," added Dr. Lund. "Six seductive bridesmaids revealing more flesh to ringside spectators than would be seemly at a masquerade ball."

"The bridesmaids dressed like courtesans, and a bride who would have blushed with shame at 16 to have her peers consider her a virgin robed and veiled like a vestal virgin," said Paul.

" 'Tis a sin to be virgin, 'tis a sin to be pure!" sang Ulla.

"The only sin recognized as sin today," said Paul soberly, "is the sin of thinking anything a sin. With regard to church weddings, Ulla, my love," he continued, "of course I believe that the wedding ceremony belongs in the church! Being married is not a private affair. It belongs to the family, the community, the church—to the church most of all, for the commitment to each other is made before God and the congregation of believers. The Roman and Greek Catholic churches regard marriage as well as Baptism and the Lord's Supper as a holy sacrament. Here I'm more Catholic than Protestant."

Ulla slipped a hand into each of their hands. "Hang on to me, or I'll float out the car window! I'm levitating with a brilliant inspiration!"

Dr. Lund promptly wrapped her long black braid around his wrist, and Paul locked his arms around her.

"Oh, you loony literalists!" she gasped. "Unhand me and listen! This will solve absolutely everything! Baptism and Holy Communion are an integral part of the Sunday morning church service. Paul, you look upon marriage as a sacrament, and I'm inclined that way, too. Why can't we simply stand up together after the post-sermon hymn and have one of your pastor friends marry us right then and there in front of the whole congregation?"

"Using the marriage service exactly as it is written in *Lutheran Book of Worship!*" cried Paul in excitement. "And the congregation won't know that they are wedding guests until we stand up together. Oh, Ulla, you are a blown-in-the-bottle genius!"

"Yes, but can she bake a wedding cake?" asked Dr. Lund.

"Indeed I can, and I will. I'll keep it covered and hidden in Henna's cab until the coffee hour after the church service, which will turn into a wedding reception."

"Please, please, not a traditional wedding cake!" pleaded Dr. Lund. "Not a dry, insipid white cake thickly covered with sickly sweet powdered-sugar frosting!"

"No frosting at all," soothed Ulla. "A dark, moist carrot cake bumpy with walnuts and raisins."

"My favorite seminary prof has a cabin on a lake off the Gunflint. I'll ask him if he can marry us. Ulla, Ulla, love of my life, can we be married next Sunday? No, I want my parents to come—and sister Maggie from New York. It will have to be the Sunday after that. How about your parents, Ulla? Will they object to such an unconventional wedding ceremony?"

"Not if it brings them a preacher son-in-law! But it is going to be hard to go back to them after that emotional leave-taking early this morning. Will you go with me, Paul? But first let's go and tell Tina and Nils. We can't keep all this a secret from them. Tina makes the best lefse I have ever tasted. And my mother makes a rye bread that belongs to cheese as much—as much as you and I belong together, Paul."

Tina and Nils were overjoyed at the news of the soon-to-be wedding. Tina, with a memory as green as the grass in May, recalled their own wedding 68 years ago.

"Was it a church wedding?" Ulla asked.

"You bet it was a church wedding," exclaimed Nils. "It was in the first St. Andrew church that I helped build. We were mighty proud of that church. How high was the steeple, Tina?"

Tina was prompt with the answer. "Sixty feet from the ground to the top. Pastor, why don't they build churches with steeples any more? A church isn't a church without a steeple."

"Ulla and I will come back and talk about that over coffee and Tina-bread sometime soon. Right now we are going to visit Ulla's grandmother at Haven Home and then go break the news to Ulla's parents. Do you think they will be able to keep the wedding a secret for two weeks?"

"Karl keep a secret?" chuckled Nils. "He's kept himself a secret all his life. Karl is the most *ordknap* person I know. What's the English for that?"

"Sparing of words. Literally, word-scanty," said Dr. Lund.

"Well, Karl Fjelstad sure is that!" exclaimed Nils. "But he was a mighty good fishing partner. He never scared the fish away with his talking."

"How did it happen?" Paul asked Ulla on the drive to Good Harbor after parting from Nils and Tina and after Toby had transported them to Paul's car. "Or *when* did it happen? I think you have told me enough so that I know how it happened. But when did your father become so silent?"

"About 25 years before I was born. I can remember the day as clearly as yesterday," she said impishly.

He bent swiftly and kissed her nose. "I deserve that! But you're an intelligent woman. You must have some idea of when your father began lapsing into silence."

"Very likely when grandpa and grandma lost their farm in the Depression and had to move back and live with great-grandmother Lissi and Erik on Cold Comfort Farm. Thanks again for that name! Grandpa died very soon after they moved back to live with great-grandmother. My father was only 12 years old. I think grandpa died of being constantly called a sonofabitch, and my father lapsed into silence from being constantly called a sonofabitch. My great-grandmother seems to have filled every room of the house with malice, so the men in the house escaped to the barn and fields—and into silence. My poor grandmother couldn't escape, so she became a cowed and frightened woman. But when great-grandmother finally died, my poor grandmother couldn't resist putting on the cloak of authority and domineering over her son and brother."

"However did such a gloomy and silent man as your father ever get married?" Paul asked.

"My mother is five years older than my father, and I'm sure she saw him as her only escape from being an old maid and went after him. When she discovered that her marriage did not justify existence or make it less bitter, she turned as cold and silent as my father."

"So you grew up in a hell of ice. I used to think hell was fire and brimstone, but I'm beginning to think that a hell of ice is a far worse hell."

"But I always had the woods and the river, Paul. Always the woods and the river. And my books. I discovered Emily Dickinson through a wonderful English teacher in high school. Can you imagine how I felt when I read her poems, Paul. They were about *me!*:

They shut me up in prose—
As when a little girl,
They put me in the closet
Because they liked me "still."

"Still!" Could themselves have peeped
And seen my brain go round,
They might as wise have lodged a bird
For treason in the pound.

"Oh, Paul," she cried suddenly as they drove into the parking lot of Haven Home. "Is it too late? Can my old grandmother, can my mother and father, ever become as dear, as wondrously dear to me as you are? Is there time yet to grow good memories of them, memories I can cherish?"

Before he opened the car door for her, he leaned on the open window and looked long and earnestly into her face. "Ulla, as a graduation gift when I graduated from college, my parents sent me to Europe for a summer. I did all the things an American is supposed to do in Europe, visited all the art museums, cathedrals. St. Peter's in Rome. Saw Michelangelo's painting in the ceiling of the Sistine Chapel of God creating Adam. The Chartres Cathedral, of course. But the most profound experience of all was of something no one had told me about—the piece of sculpture high in the north portal of the Chartres Cathedral, the sculpture of Christ creating the *new* Adam. To me it is even greater than Michelangelo's painting. Ulla, all day you have been calling this the first day of your life. Do you not believe that Christ can do for them what he did for you?"

"I believe," she said softly. "Help me when I unbelieve."

When they entered the old woman's room, it was quite obvious that there was not going to be much time left for growing cherishable memories. The hands resting on the white bedspread looked more like the withered claws of a dead blue heron than like human hands. The skin on her corded neck and death-mask face was like parchment. Only her eyes, dark as black currants, were mobile, restlessly roving and shifting with her capricious memories, no longer anchored to calendared time.

Ulla went to the bedside and took the clawlike hand into her own. "Hello, grandma. It's Ulla."

"Ulla who?" the sunken mouth croaked.

"Ulla, your granddaughter."

"I s'pose you're blaming me, too, 'cause the currant jelly didn't jell!"

"No, grandma, I don't blame you for anything."

"It spun a thread just as she said it should, but still it didn't jell, and she's so mad she's fit to be tied."

The cords in the withered neck jerked with sobs. Paul stepped swiftly to the bedside and placed his hand on the old woman's head.

"Helga, dear," he said soothingly, "the jelly is going to jell. It's standing in the sun on the windowsill. It's beautiful, Helga, and it's slowly but surely jelling."

The old woman's eyes grew bright with recognition. "Pastor, it's *you!*"

"Does she recognize you?" Ulla asked in amazement.

"She thinks I'm my great-grandfather."

"So it's you, Pastor. And this girl is your beautiful Maggie! She *is* beautiful, Pastor, and I'm glad for you. I really am glad for you, Pastor!"

The mobile eyes in the parchment face smiled at both

of them, but suddenly filled with terror. She clutched their hands frantically. "Don't eat the blueberries! There's poison berries in them. She put them there. She put the poison berries in with the berries you picked. I know it for sure! Don't eat them! You'll die! I don't want you to die-e-e!"

Her voice rose to a shriek. Two nurse's aides came running. "You had better leave. We'll give her a sedative."

Paul touched Ulla's elbow and guided her in silence to the car, but she did not get in.

"So that is how it was," she said quietly. "That is how your great-grandparents died!"

"Please, Ulla! Your grandmother is a very confused woman. She doesn't know what she is saying!"

"My grandmother is finally telling the truth that has haunted her all her life. Her mother—my great-grandmother, Paul—murdered your great-grandparents. My horrible great-grandmother murdered your wonderful great-grandparents!"

"Ulla, I refuse to believe a senile old woman's—"

"Paul!" she said sharply, and he was silent.

"Please take me back to my car," she said and climbed into his.

They drove in silence to his cabin.

When they parted, she did not touch him, but looked steadily and pleadingly into his eyes. "I am not now as I was before, Paul. I will never be that person again. There *was* a miracle. I believe it, and you must believe it, too. I thank God and you for that. I love you. I will always love you. But I cannot marry you. There will always be that double murder between us. No, please don't say anything. There is nothing to say."

Because he knew it was true, he silently stepped back from the bright orange pickup and let it drive away. There was nothing more for either one of them to say. Nothing to do.

Fourteen

Paul found them drinking tea at his kitchen table when conscientiousness about his as yet unfinished Sunday sermon won over his grief and despair about Ulla and maneuvered him into the cabin. At this moment the presence of any human beings would be painful. Why, then, this rude, vulgar couple that had tried to provoke him at the community Fourth of July picnic at the public dock? They looked so damnably smug sitting there drinking his tea from the mugs Maggie had made for him when she was slightly potty about becoming a potter. Annoyance, multiplied to the point of explosion by fatigue and grief, struggled with the disposition he had been rigorously disciplining to accept any and all interruptions in a Christian spirit of love. Sarcasm lost the struggle. "Good evening! I'm happy to see that you have made yourselves at home," Paul said.

"You weren't here, so we decided to come in and wait for you," the girl replied.

"After all, it's your job as a preacher to keep open house and be hospitable," the young man added. "That's what you're paid for."

"Hospitality of house and home and heart is not restricted to the clergy. I know many lay people who practice it," said Paul evenly. "Perhaps you would be so hospitable as to welcome me home with a mug of tea and cheese and crackers. Ah, I see you have already found the cheese and crackers. Rather excellent cheese, don't you think? I imagine that you two also prefer a grown-up cheese. Would you like to move into the living room? Incidentally, what are your names?"

"I'm Nick, and she's Della. This isn't exactly a social visit, you know. We've come to be married. Della's pregnant. I wanted her to get rid of the kid, but she doesn't want to. I've got the marriage license here in my pocket."

"I must admit to being somewhat surprised," said Paul after a pause. "I would imagine that you two would prefer to be married at the courthouse by a justice of the peace rather than by a pastor."

"It's your job to marry people free," Nick muttered. "We would have had to pay a justice of the peace a fee."

"I also have the right to refuse to marry people if I suspect that they hold the marriage in contempt."

"Please don't think he's as mean and callous as he sounds," pleaded the girl, the hint of tears in her eyes. "He really wants the baby, too. You see, we're both PKs—preachers' kids, that is—and if we're going to be married, we want it to mean a little more than just a legal contract."

"But apparently not mean so much that you want to be married in a church in the presence of your families," Paul said.

"Christ, no!" said Nick vehemently.

"I'm not surprised that you are PKs," said Paul. "Preachers' kids are so overexposed to the gospel that sometimes some of them have violent responses to it—violently negative or violently positive. But, Nick and Della, you do need a witness to your marriage. When people come all unexpected and ask to be married privately, the pastor usually brings in his spouse as a witness. I have no spouse, so may I call my friend Dr. Lund and ask him to come over? He's the closest, except for Nils and Tina Larson, who, no doubt, are getting ready for bed by now."

While they were waiting for Dr. Lund to arrive, Paul brewed another pot of tea and took a tin of brownies out of the freezer compartment of the refrigerator.

"Before we conduct this marriage ceremony," he said, "I must warn you that I do have a fee. No, Nick, you don't have to give me any money. You have to give of your selves. I suspect that you came up here to the wilderness for the same reason some others are coming up here these days—to get away from the human mass and mess and to live utterly by and for and with themselves. It's true that people living that sort of life don't run the risk of unhappy or tragic human relationships, but they run a risk of a far more tragic relationship to their own beings. My fee is that you begin giving of yourselves to others. By the time your baby comes, you will then be much more able to give yourselves to your child. I respect you for saying no to abortion and yes to life. In so doing, like it or not, you are saying yes to God."

"At least you don't demand that we go to your church," mumbled Nick.

"I would never demand church attendance of anyone, Nick. Attendance at church comes when a person begins to experience such joy in a love affair with God and fellow beings that he or she simply can't stay away. But I hear Toby's steps on the gravel. Excuse me while I go to my study and find the Lutheran marriage ceremony."

The same ceremony Ulla and I were going to have—and now it may never be—and now those two will have it, he thought with a pang.

Dr. Lund, true to his Swedish love of candles, had brought along two six-branched candelabra, which he lit and placed on opposite sides of the mantle on the capacious stone fireplace. "I can't imagine a wedding without candles," he said.

Paul, true to his love of Bach, played "Jesu, Joy of Man's Desiring" on the stereo. "I can't imagine a wedding without Bach. In this piece he exults as only Bach can in the source of all love and the object of all human love and desiring."

"I wish you could cut the stagey stuff," muttered Nick sullenly.

"Nicholas, my friend," said Paul firmly. "You are facing an existential either/or. Either this marriage ceremony is my way, or it's the justice-of-the-peace way."

An hour later Paul and Dr. Lund sat alone in the candlelight of one candelabrum. The newly wedded pair had left, meekly silenced by Toby's impulsive gift of the other candelabrum and Paul's of the Bach record. Paul had blessed them at the door with the Aaronic blessing: "The Lord bless you and keep you; the Lord make his face shine upon you and be gracious to you; the Lord lift up his countenance upon you and give you peace." To this he added his own blessing: "May you fall in love with God and in that love learn to love each other all the more and all others as well. In that love of God may you learn to serve each other and others more. In that love may you receive your child as a gift. And may you reverence and remember this wedding night more with each passing year. May you joyfully celebrate it in the year 2000 with your united families! Goodnight, PKs!"

After Paul had told Dr. Lund about what had happened in Helga's room at Haven Home and Ulla's sober announcement that she could never marry the great-grandson of the man and woman her great-grandmother had murdered, the two men sat in a long silence. The candles flickered in the breeze that came through the screen door.

Dr. Lund finally broke the silence. "I can certainly understand her decision as a first reaction to what must have been for her a horrifying revelation. Give her a few days, and maybe she will be willing to talk about it and reconsider. Perhaps you can convince her that what her great-grandmother in all probability did in no way affects the relationship between you two. With your permission I'll go to her in my self-appointed role as a discerner of souls and tell her that I do not discern a shadow of a change in your love for her after her grandmother's disclosure of her lifelong terrifying suspicions. Will you let me try?"

"It won't work, Toby. Ulla's last words to me were 'Please don't say anything. There is nothing to say.' She is right, Toby. Neither you nor I nor any mortal being can say anything to her in this darkness. In this darkness I cannot be her light. Indeed, I am part of this new darkness that has come upon her. This is a total darkness, total despair, and she is all alone in it."

"My God! Is it that bad?"

"It's that bad!" Paul replied.

"What do we do? Nothing?"

"Sometimes doing nothing is the hardest thing to do—and the only thing to do. We shall do nothing, Toby, but wait."

"Wait for what?"

"Wait for the unexpected."

"Waiting has never been my strong point!" sighed Dr. Lund.

"Nor mine, but when one becomes involved with God, one begins to realize one's weaknesses. I suppose that's to make us lean a little harder on him."

The two sat in silence again, listening to the waves splashing rhythmically against the shore.

"It hurts me to think of Ulla all alone in her despair," said Dr. Lund. "As small and defenseless now as when she was a child craving love and laughter and talk and was deprived of them, finding her only happiness in nature and books."

"This is not the same, Toby. She is not as defenseless and deprived as when she was a child. She knows that I love her. Early this morning something unexpected and miraculous happened to her, and she became convinced of God's love. I was wrong when I said that she is in total despair and all alone in it. She is not alone, and she knows it. Her problem now is to forgive. Forgive her great-grandmother. Forgive her grandparents. Forgive her parents. She needs to be healed of all hatred and anger and bitterness toward them."

"It's a monstrous thing to forgive. Now that you can guess what happened, have you forgiven, Paul?"

"My primary feeling now is the same it has always been—deep gratitude to those relatives in Kandiyohi county who fetched my orphaned grandfather from

Good Harbor, took him into their home and family, and satisfied his human hunger for love and laughter and talk. As for Ulla's great-grandmother, my first reaction to the revelation that she had murdered my great-grandparents was rage and yes, hatred—but now I feel only a great pity for her. By the way, have you figured out what happened, Sherlock? What were those seeds you found on the shelf in the cellar of the old house?"

"Just what I expected—the seeds of the water hemlock, *Cicuta bulbifera*, a deadly poisonous plant. The seeds are very small and inconspicuous and could easily be mixed into a bowl of blueberries, or any other food for that matter. Covered with thick Jersey cream, they would be undetected by unsuspecting eyes and taste-buds. Lissi used the blue-bead lily berries, which also are poisonous, to make people think that your great-grandparents mistook them for blueberries. She used the water hemlock seeds to be sure that the bowl of blueberries would be lethal. Her daughter Helga knew nothing about poison seeds, but she has carried to this day the horrible suspicion that her mother put those blue-bead berries into the bowls of blueberries and cream your great-grandparents ate and the pail of berries they took home with them. Helga was intelligent enough to know that Pastor Poul Amundson and his wife would never confuse those berries."

"Why did she do it?" Paul asked. "Premeditated murder requires a colossal hatred."

"Which that woman, according to Nils and Tina, had to a monstrous degree. My life has been concerned with people's bodies, and I haven't meddled much with their minds. Something in that woman's life must have terribly twisted her mind. A good number of people live by the principle of hating most those who are nearest—

nearest members of the family, nearest neighbors. She apparently lived by that principle, almost demonically, but could make a good pretense of covering it up if she wanted to. She would refuse to go to the funerals of some neighbors and would lavish baked and canned goods on others, but hated them all. She seemed to hate men most, especially men she considered weaklings— her husband, for example, and the man Helga married. But she admired your great-grandfather, saw that he was a bit attracted to Helga that first summer, and pinned all her hopes on his coming back as a bachelor pastor and courting her daughter. Well, he came back with a wife and baby, and that was too bitter a pill for her to take."

"For the first time I think I understand Luther's conclusion to the Ten Commandments," said Paul. "It used to bother me to think of the curse of a father's sin extending to the third and fourth generations. But it does indeed! And the mother's as well, although Luther didn't say anything about that."

"Or the curse of the parents' non-sins," said Toby. "Some day I'll tell you about the damage I've seen that has been done to children by spotless and undefiled parents."

"The only way these curses can be cancelled," continued Paul, "is by forgiveness. Now, however, I think I had better go to bed so that you can go home, as the old couple said to their guests when they stayed too long."

"Like Dickens' Mr. Finching, a most estimable man, to whom it was only necessary to mention asparagus and it appeared, or to hint at any delicate thing to drink and it came like magic. I don't need a hint as broad as that," laughed Dr. Lund. "Good night, and may you sleep well!"

"Before you go, Toby, I have a favor to ask of you. It would be wonderful to honeymoon under a full moon. The moon is full a week from Sunday. Could Ulla and I borrow your canoe for a week to go camping in the Boundary Waters?"

"So you are still expecting the unexpected?"

"Perhaps it is more correct to say that I am turning the healing of Ulla over to the Lord. I trust and believe that he has some fantastic way to do it tucked up his sleeve."

Fifteen

The sermon for the Eighth Sunday after Pentecost practically wrote itself the next morning after the phrase "the oil of tenderness and the wine of compassion" unexpectedly leaped into his mind. The good Samaritan had bandaged the wounds of the man beaten up by robbers and left half dead and had poured oil and wine on them. "The oil of tenderness and the wine of compassion!" The phrase bubbled up again and again in his sermon like the sparkling bubbles in champagne.

The oil of tenderness and the wine of compassion—to pour on all the wounded ones of the world. All the victims of human hatred—race hatred, class hatred, neighbor hatred, congregation hatred, family hatred. The oil of tenderness and the wine of compassion—to pour on Grandmother Helga's first-generation wounds, on Ulla's father's second-generation wounds, on Ulla's third-generation wounds.

The oil of tenderness and the wine of compassion—the only elements that can penetrate the sealed-in pain and bitterness of old unhealed wounds. Wounds that have taken on an obstinacy of their own and refuse to be healed. Wounds that fester and cause the wounded ones themselves to become wounders.

And where does one get that miraculous oil and wine that can do the impossible, can heal the unhealable wounds? From where does one receive the strength of mind, the strength of heart, the strength of soul that are symbolized by the oil of tenderness and the wine of compassion?

To answer these rhetorical questions, Paul would read once again the Epistle lesson, which ended with: "May you be strengthened with all power, according to his glorious might. . . . He has delivered us from the dominion of darkness and transferred us to the kingdom of his beloved Son, in whom we have redemption, the forgiveness of sins."

Forgiveness, Ulla, my wounded one! This sermon is for you! Paul thought. *Here in this Gospel and Epistle are the oil of tenderness and the wine of compassion for your wounds. Please come to St. Andrew tomorrow—even if you are thinking this is the last time you will ever come!*

There were so many summer tourists in church on Sunday that chairs had to be placed in the aisles and entrance, but Ulla and her parents were not there. Had she run away again, then? Paul wondered. Climbed into Henna, still packed with all her worldly goods, and left the Shore forever? Out of all reach? Out of all touch? And he had written this sermon just for her! Ah, was he still perhaps relying on his own powers of communication and persuasion? When would he be healed of his lack of total trust and faith in God? When would he

strip himself of all confidence in his own self and sur-
render his will to God's will? When would he be able to
stand still and let God do what had to be done?

Paul stepped into the pulpit, opened the Bible to the
Gospel lesson in the 10th chapter of Luke, and looked
down into the faces looking up at him expectantly. The
lives of most of these people had very likely been bound
up with the church since childhood. Had they already
sucked all the good out of this old story? But if the truths
of this parable had really registered something good on
their minds and hearts, why, then, did they continue
to hate and hurt and wound each other as they did?
Why did they continue to be so engrossed in their own
wounds and be so indifferent to the open and obvious
wounds of others? Of course these people needed to
hear this old parable again!

After a long and almost embarrassing pause, Paul
leaned across the pulpit and spoke as if he were speaking
to each one individually. "Are you sick and tired to death
of hearing this old parable? Is it as familiar to your ears
as the story of Goldilocks and the Three Bears? Are you
hoping that I will jazz it up a little and make it contemporary? At least do that to this old story you're probably
fed up with hearing? Turn the priest into a Lutheran
pastor on his way to the monthly meeting of the Min-
isterial Association. Turn the Levite into the Chairman
of the Board of Trustees, late for a committee meeting
on the sale of the parsonage. Turn the good Samaritan
into an Indian on his way from the Reservation to Good
Harbor to buy a spare tire. Have the Indian use the
money for the spare tire on behalf of the poor victim of
an attack by a gang of drunken ruffians. Is that what
you expect? Or want?

"I grant that it would be refreshing to hear this old parable freshened up a little. But would that really do anything for your inner being? Christ's concern when he told that story in the first place was with the inner being of the young lawyer who asked him what he had to do to inherit eternal life. Christ's concern today is exactly the same as it was then—with the inner being of each and every individual. This ancient parable concerns your inner being and mine. Whoever you are and wherever you come from, this story that you may find tiresome and outworn has something to say to you and to me. Or rather, it has something to *ask* you and me.

"What does the story of the good Samaritan ask you and me? Is it possible, it asks you and me, is it possible for you and me to help heal the wounded persons we find on the road of life? Is it possible for you and me, who ourselves are wounded and suffering from hurt and bitter feelings, inherited or self-willed alienations, old or new grudges and jealousies—is it possible for us to enter into the mystery of God's healing?

"The good Samaritan poured oil and wine on the wounds of the victim of human violence. Can you and I, who ourselves are in some way victims of some human violence or other—and violence, I need not remind you, can be mental and spiritual as well as physical—can you and I pour the oil of tenderness and the wine of compassion on another's wounds?

"Brothers and sisters in Christ, can we here in St. Andrew Church form a community of compassion, a community that lives in Christ's forgiveness and therefore can forgive? Can we form a community of compassion that shares another's pain, becomes part of another's pain? Is it possible for old wounds that have never been healed to be healed by the oil of tenderness and the wine of compassion? Is it possible for members of St. Andrew Church to live together in loving forgiveness, growing each day in love, being patient with each other's faults and frailties, helping each other gently, peacefully, constantly? Is it possible?"

Putting aside his prepared sermon, he talked on and on, heedless of time, until Dr. Lund stood up in the second row of pews and interrupted him. "Forgive the interruption, Pastor, but if the congregation at Good Harbor is to hear this wonderful sermon, you had better get on the road this minute. You can still make it without breaking the speed limit."

Paul looked at his wristwatch and clapped his hands to his head. His peal of laughter released an antiphony of giggles and laughs that followed him as he made his way through the crowded aisle. He stopped momentarily at the door and turned back to them. "Please begin the application of the sermon you just heard by forgiving me for being so long-winded!"

When he returned to his cabin about one o'clock, he found a note stuck to his screen door from Dr. Lund, asking him to call Tina and Nils immediately.

"Ya, Pastor, Tina and I heard at coffee hour in church this morning that Helga is dyin'," Nils said over the phone. "That's why Karl and Olga and Ulla weren't in church this morning. We thought you would like to know."

"Indeed I do! I shall go back to Good Harbor at once."

On a sudden impulse Paul asked Nils if they happened to have a Norwegian Bible and hymnbook. Nils was sure that they had the Norwegian Bible, because they read together out of it sometimes, but he wasn't so sure about the Norwegian hymnbook and called Tina to the phone.

"Ya, Pastor, we have *Landstads Salmebog,*" Tina said. "It's the hymnbook we sang out of in the olden days."

"Does it have the communion service?"

"Ya, shure!"

"Would you put a marker on the page of the communion service? I'll be there in five minutes to pick up the Bible and the hymnbook."

At Haven Home he found the usual brigade of patients in wheelchairs in the lobby, some waiting hopefully for Sunday afternoon visitors, some watching hopelessly the comings and goings in the bitter knowledge that no one would come to see them. Others, whose minds were blank to either hope or hopelessness, sat vacantly staring into nothing.

Today Paul did not stop to greet them individually, but gave them a cheery collective salute and strode down the east corridor to Helga's door, which unlike the others in the hallway was closed. He knocked lightly and waited.

Ulla opened the door only enough to reveal her fatigued face. Her eyes widened and swiftly registered the shift of her conflicting emotions. Surprise, joy, alarm, and dismay chased each other on and off her face. "You should not have come," she said in a low voice. "We must not see each other any more."

"Ulla," he said firmly, "this is a pastoral visit. It has nothing to do with you and me."

"Thank you for coming, Pastor," she whispered, and opened the door wide.

He searched her face for traces of mockery, but found none. Was it genuine relief he detected in her eyes, as if she now could shift a heavy burden from her shoulders to his? *Ulla, my love, I take it gladly!* he thought.

Karl and Olga sat wooden-straight in the two determinedly and designedly cheerful plastic armchairs by the windows overlooking the lake. Plastic! Paul's capricious mind leaped crazily to the thought that their faces described precisely what had happened to the word *plastic*. At one time it had meant soft, yielding, moldable, pliable, capable of being formed and molded. Now the word had taken on the meaning of the hardened synthetic material that was incapable of being molded. Ulla's parents were plastic people—forlorn and frozen, stripped of the possibility of taking on any other quality than this dreadful and doleful heaviness.

Fie on the thought! Paul said to himself. *Where there is life there is hope. Even in the eleventh hour. Even at five minutes until midnight. Even for this 93-year-old woman a shallow breath or two from death.* He shook hands gravely with the two, wondering as he did so if they had any conception of how hopelessly and yet hopefully he was in love with their daughter. *Have they ever really been in love with each other?* he wondered.

"She's taking her time at it," said Ulla's mother, almost plaintively, although her face showed no more expression than a dust mop.

"In many ways deathing is like birthing," he said. "For some it goes swiftly and easily. For others it drags out and is a long struggle."

He turned from the parents to the bed. Helga's bright dark eyes that on Friday had darted here and there like a nervous bird's were tightly closed. Only her chest moved as her lungs stubbornly and convulsively fought for the breath of life. He had been at enough deathbeds already to know the meaning of breath. Ulla pushed a chair close to the bed for him, but Paul moved it aside and knelt close to Helga's head. "I want to be as close to her ear as possible," he said.

"The doctor says that she sees nothing, hears nothing, knows nothing," Ulla replied.

"Doctors are sometimes wrong. God willing, she may hear what we say. Hearing is the last sense to go."

"And touch. She does seem to know that I am holding her hand and seems to feel comforted. I have been holding it all night long."

Paul reached for Helga's other hand and gently stroked it. He leaned closer to her ear and spoke slowly, distinctly. "Helga, you are not alone. Your son Karl is here. Your daughter-in-law Olga is here. Your granddaughter Ulla is here. I am here. I am the new pastor at St. Andrew. We are all here with you, Helga. You are not alone."

There was no response, no change in the intervals between the noisy, labored breaths. Ulla's eyes filled with tears, and she silently shook her head at Paul.

Ulla, my love, he thought, *you do not believe. You once asked me to help you in your unbelief. Believe with me now in this moment, Ulla. Believe!*

"Helga, Ulla is holding one of your hands. I am holding the other. Helga, if you hear me, please squeeze our hands."

Her hands continued to rest in theirs like dead bones in a shrivelled casing.

Karl shifted his chair impatiently as if to tell them to stop this nonsense.

Suddenly Paul knew why he had bothered to stop at Nil's and Tina's to pick up the Norwegian Bible and hymnbook. Without removing the hand that held Helga's he reached for the books and propped them against the diminuitive ridge Helga's body made under the sheet. With his left hand he fumbled until he found the table of contents in the Norwegian Bible. Slowly pausing between each word, he began to read the names of the books of the Old Testament: *"Første Mosebog, Anden Mosebog, Tredje Mosebog, Fjerde Mosebog—"*

There was a convulsive movement in the shrivelled claws, and guttural sounds formed behind the deep hollows in Helga's throat. Not the syllables of *Femte Mosebog,* but the cadences.

"Oh, Paul, she hears you!" whispered Ulla, her dark eyes luminous with joy. "Go on! Go on!"

"Josuasbog, Dommernes bog," continued Paul, then stopped and waited. This time the sounds that emerged were clearly syllables.

"Rooooots Bog—"

"Første Samuelsbog," said Paul.

"Anden Sam-u-elsbog," spoke Helga hoarsely, and then ever more clearly, *"Forste Kong-e-bog, Anden Kong-e-bog—"*

"Wonderful, Helga! Now can you open your eyes, Helga? Open your eyes and look at us!"

Karl and Olga slid their chairs closer to the bed and leaned intently forward. All four watched as the mind fought to unite with the body again and assume the control that had been lost so long. Ulla placed Helga's hand against her breast as if she were trying to pour all her own strength into the dying woman so that she could lift the weight of her eyelids. Helga struggled to tear her eyelids apart, succeeded once, but then closed them again under their sheer weight.

She's slipping back, Paul thought. *She mustn't. She mustn't!* He reached for the Norwegian hymnbook.

What was the name of the man who had written one of the most beautiful and meaningful of all hymns? His grandfather had once told him, in fact in their evening devotions had sung his German hymns in their Norwegian translation. What was his name? Paul Gerhardt! Was it in Landstad's hymnbook? Paul searched frantically. Where would it be—in the Easter section? No, it was an Advent hymn. His grandfather had sung it in Advent. Ah, here it was! His grandfather's favorite hymn, and it could be Helga's too! He would sing it to her, sing every stanza. *"Spirit of the Living Word," I know the tune. Help me with the words!* Paul prayed silently.

> *Hvorledes skal jeg møde*
> *Og ære dig, min Skat?*

He sang each stanza, and by the time he reached the third one, he strongly sensed the meaning and could make the strange words eloquent.

> *Hvor har du, milde Hjerte,*
> *Dog ingen Møie spart,*
> *At dæmpe al den Smerte,*
> *Som klemte mig saa hart!*
> *Da jeg i Mørkheds Sæde*
> *Og Dodens Skygger sad,*
> *Da kom du selv, min Glæde,*
> *Og gjorde mig saa glad.*

When he had sung the hymn through, all 10 stanzas, he took Helga's hand in his again and spoke slowly into her ear. "He is coming, Helga. He is coming to take away all your pain and turn all your darkness into light."

A faint flush of lifeblood showed through the lifeless skin stretched over Helga's high cheekbones. The eyelids opened again, this time effortlessly, as if from a

refreshing sleep. They were deep and dark and cloud-
less, cleansed of all anxiety. They looked first at him,
then at Ulla, moved to Olga, and finally rested on Karl,
who suddenly slipped out of his chair, knelt beside Ulla,
took his mother's hand from her and held it in his own.

"*Mor*," he stammered, as if his vocal cords were rusty
from not having said the word for decades.

"Karl! *Min Karl!*" she murmured, as if she had always
pronounced that name in deepest love. When he felt her
hand tug, Paul quickly released it. She raised both her
arms to Karl, and he went into them without embar-
rassment, although he turned his face into Helga's pillow
to hide his tears. Ulla slipped her arm around his shoulders. Olga's look of bafflement slowly changed to won-
derment. She knelt awkwardly beside Ulla, whose other
arm now went around her shoulders. Paul engraved the
picture before him deeply on his soul lest he later might
disbelieve his mind's memory of it.

Oh, you Soul-Repairer, forgive my lapses of faith! Paul
prayed. *I didn't quite believe that you could do it! You have
cleansed and cleared Helga for eternity. Now finish what you
have begun with these three. Help me not to bungle your work!*

Leaving the three kneeling beside the bed, he swiftly
found a nurse's aide and asked for a loaf of bread and
a cup. He took out of his briefcase the bottle of wine he
always carried for giving Holy Communion to the bedridden and homebound people that he visited.

At the bedside again, he could perceive that Helga,
despite the contented look on her face, would very soon
slip back again into a coma.

"Helga, Karl, Olga, and Ulla," he said. "I would like
us to take Holy Communion together before Helga goes
to sleep, perhaps to awaken again only in eternity. Christ

has been present in this room today. He has clearly shown us that lives that have been heavy and difficult can be miraculously changed in a few minutes, even face-to-face with death. It is a mystery, the mystery of faith, faith in Christ, faith in the power of his death on the cross and his resurrection, faith in the power of God's forgiveness. By this mystery Helga has been freed. She knows herself forgiven. She is not afraid to die. This is the moment in the lives of the four of us to turn to God and ask to be healed from our own fear of trusting him and trusting in each other, to be healed of our own lack of faith. I am convinced that this is a new beginning for the four of us and that from this hour we four will grow in love of God and trust in him and in love and trust of each other. So let us celebrate this mystery and miracle by taking communion together, asking God to forgive us all our sins and to forgive each other.

"Because Helga is very tired, we will dispense with the liturgy. I shall just read what I think is the Norwegian Agnus Dei that Tina marked in the hymnbook, and then we will receive the body and blood of Jesus Christ. Karl, I will dip a morsel of the bread into the cup of wine, and you will hold it to your mother's lips. Only for her to touch it is enough."

Holding in his hands the cup of wine he had poured out, Paul read from the hymnbook:

"O Guds Lam uskyldig
Paa Korset ihjelslaget,
Indtil Døden lydig,
Hvor ilde du var plaget,
For vor Skyld var du saaret,
Har Verdens Synder baaret
Miskund' dig over os, o Jesus!

Miskund' dig over os, o Jesus!
Giv os din Fred, o Herre Jesus!"

Paul dipped a morsel of bread into the cup of wine and gave it to Karl, who held it to his mother's lips.

"Helga," said Paul, placing his hand on her head, "this is Christ's body and blood, given for you and for us for the forgiveness of sins."

Faintly, ever so faintly they heard Helga whisper, *"Herre Gud, himmelske Fader! Jeg takker dig. Amen!"*

When Paul gave the bread and wine to Karl, Olga, and Ulla, he boldly stretched the pronouncement of forgiveness backward in time. "Karl, Olga, and Ulla," he said, "this is Christ's body and blood, given for you and for me for the forgiveness of sins, all of our sins, all of yours and all of mine, and all the sins of our ancestors, whatever they may have been, however wicked and malignant they may have been."

"Ulla," he said when they had received the bread and wine from his hands, "will you in Christ's name and in the Lutheran belief in the priesthood of all believers give me Holy Communion?"

If she was startled, she did not betray it. She gravely took the cup and the bread from his hands. He stood before her and reached out his cupped hand for the bread.

Did the cup of wine tremble as she held it up to his lips? But her voice did not tremble when she pronounced the forgiveness of his sins. "Paul," she said, "this is Christ's body and blood, given for you and for me for the forgiveness of sins, all of your sins and all of mine, and all the sins of our ancestors, whatever they may have been, however wicked and malignant they may have been!"

After he had drunk from the cup, Paul said, "We will close with the Lord's Prayer. If you can pray it in Norwegian, Karl and Olga, please do so. I have it here in the Norwegian hymnbook. Ulla, will you try to pray it with me in Norwegian?"

Once again Helga's vocal cords found the cadence of the familiar prayer, but the sounds that issued forth became more and more guttural. By the Amen her eyes were tightly closed.

"Thanks be to God, she will soon depart in peace," Paul said. "And thanks be to you, Karl and Olga and Ulla, for helping to give her this peaceful departure. And now I think I should leave you three alone. May the peace of God, which passes all understanding, keep your hearts and minds and my heart and mind in Christ Jesus."

Before they could say anything, Paul was out the door and gone. Sooner or later Henna would arrive at his door, of that he was absolutely convinced.

When Henna finally did arrive about ten o'clock that night, he did not go out, but stood by the window, waiting and watching the new moon over the lake. It was not full yet, but after next Sunday it would be resplendently full.

Ulla's arms encircled him from behind, and he turned in the circle of them and held her hungrily to himself.

"I really came on two urgent errands," she said after a time. "First to thank Pastor for his pastoral call and report to him that grandmother died very peacefully an hour ago. My parents hope that Pastor can conduct the funeral next Wednesday. They want her to be buried in the family lot in the old cemetery where your great-grandparents are buried."

"*Oldefar* and *oldemor* would approve of those arrangements, I am sure. And the second urgent errand?"

"I came to ask the man I am going to marry to call his parents and sister and the professor who is going to marry us and anyone else that should come to make all the necessary arrangements to come to St. Andrew by church time next Sunday."

"Your obedient servant!" Paul said, releasing her and moving to the phone in the little room he had converted into his study. By the time he had made his various calls and explained to somewhat amazed and overwhelmed relatives and friends the whys and whens and wheres and came back into the living room, he found Ulla sound asleep on the couch. When he covered her with a light blanket, she moved her head slightly, and the end of her thick black braid tumbled to the braided rug and lay in the light of the quarter moon.

"Christ has redeemed and altered our pasts, my love," he whispered. "And one week from tonight Creator God will fill the night sky with a full moon and trillions of stars. All for you and for me!"